Sparks of Affection

~Men of the Heart: Book Two~

Steve C. Roberts

Also By Steve C. Roberts

Non-fiction

One Minute Thoughts: A Daily Devotional
Mighty Men: Lessons for the Christian Soldier
Seven Steps to the Successful Christian Life

Fiction

~Men of the Heart Series~
Kindled Love – Book 1
Sparks of Affection – Book 2
Flames of Endearment – Book 3
Light of Devotion – Book 4
Look for Book 5 in 2021

Flight Cancelled: A Christmas Romance
A Walk in the Park: A Christmas Romance
(Coming in 2020)

Young Adult Fiction

~New Age of Hunters Series~
Hunted: On the Run – Book 1
Hunted: Hunters and Hunted – Book 2

The Killing Field

ISBN-13: 978-1503331938

ISBN-10: 1503331938

This work would not have happened without the support of many people; but specific thanks to Elizabeth for keeping this story grounded in reality; and to Meghan, my number one fan.

Thanks for being there with encouragement every step of the way.

Finally, a word to the readers who encouraged this story to continue.

Thank you.

Table of Contents

Prologue

Catherine walked quickly down the cobbled street, heading for home. Something felt off today. People were acting... off, and she didn't know why.

It started at Mavis' clothing shop, where some of the ladies were whispering while looking at her. She had shrugged that off, remembering the lesson her father had taught her about assuming things. The problem was that it kept up. Through the next two places she stopped there were whispers and pointing.

"And how is Alfred today?"

Startled, she looked over. Mrs. Winthrop was in her yard, staring hard, a strange look in her eye.

"Oh, hello Mrs. Winthrop." She called lightly. She wondered why she would ask about Alfred. "I haven't seen Alfred since Church Sunday."

"Well, you're not likely to see him very soon then." With that, she turned and marched toward her house.

Catherine recoiled, wondering what was wrong with people today. She hurried home, not stopping to talk to anyone else, and entered the house, breathless. As she came through the sitting room, she was surprised to see her father in a chair, talking with a policeman. Concerned, she stopped, "What's wrong, father?"

Her father looked up at her and shook his head. "Sit down, Catherine. We need to talk about Alfred..."

Chapter One

The air in the crowded coach was stifling. Catherine waved the fan harder, willing the coach to start moving again soon. She was pressed between a matronly woman in blue and a very smelly businessman who had spent the last fifteen miles trying to explain to her the dangers of frontier life for a single woman. She hoped he wasn't working up to a proposal. It wasn't the type of memory she wanted for her second one. Her first one was a poor enough memory.

"...so the woman that I marry will be well off, once I get my business rolling. I just need a few..."

The coach titled slightly as the large woman leaned forward, a menacing look on her face. "Will you stop bothering this poor girl! She is too polite to tell you to shut up, but I'm not."

The businessman stared wide eyed in unbelief for a few seconds before sputtering a response, "Well... I never..."

"Now you have, so be quiet. She's not giving you money and she is not going to marry you either."

Catherine mouthed a silent 'thank you' to the woman, who smiled and patted her leg. "If he bothers you any more I'll have him thrown off the coach. He can walk back."

The man sputtered for a moment more, and then fell abruptly silent as the woman glared one last time. Satisfied, she sat back in her seat and closed her eyes.

Turning her head slightly to hide her smile, Catherine continued to wave the fan, angling it slightly to give the woman some of the breeze.

Just then the coach finally started to move. Catherine couldn't believe how long it was taking to get to her sister's town. Her sister had moved west several years ago with her husband, Theodore, and set up a home in the middle of nowhere. Theodore's brother had come up with a grand idea to start a town, so they pooled their money and started one centered around a store. They named their town Cobbinsville, after Theodore and Frederick's last name, Cobbins. She had laughed at the name when her sister's letter had arrived explaining how they founded a town. It seemed kind of... conceited, to give a town your own name.

The town was founded anyway, and had been for a couple of years. Fred died last winter, so now it was Ted's, and her sister Elizabeth's, of course.

She hoped the ride wouldn't take much longer. She had never had to ride this long to go anywhere back east. Closing her eyes, she wondered what all of her friends thought of her leaving. After Alfred had been arrested for stealing from his work she had been so ashamed. Breaking off their engagement hadn't been enough, she had to leave town.

When Elizabeth's letter had arrived and mentioned her coming out, it had seemed like a wonderful opportunity.

The stage jolted violently, throwing the passengers against each other.

"Sorry," The teamster hollered from outside. *"Rock in the trail."*

Straightening herself in her seat, Catherine had to roll her eyes. Some wonderful opportunity; the chance to get thrown into smelly sweaty people on a 12 hour stage ride.

The teamster's voice sounded out again, *"Town's ahead, people. About ten more minutes."*

Relieved, she sat a tad straighter. She couldn't wait to see her sister.

****

James clicked his tongue, urging the horse to move a little faster. It was hot out. He could feel the sweat running down his back as he rode, and couldn't wait to get out of the sun.

He had been riding all morning. The Church was planning a social that was coming up in a few weeks, and Parson Stone had put him on the committee. He hated committees, almost as much as he hated riding a few hours to get a simple question answered. He had to run all the way out to Parson's ranch to ask about music.

He pulled his kerchief from his pocket and mopped the sweat from his face. It didn't matter, it had been a good visit, and he was almost back to town anyway. He had a nice gourd full of cool water hanging in his office, waiting for him to drink.

He liked his job. He had grown up in this area; his Pa had come west and settled here in the 1830's, back when it was empty and desolate. When he was growing up the nearest town had been Grover, a few dozen miles south of his Pa's ranch. When the railroad planned to put the tracks over fifty miles north, the town just died, and people moved away.

Cobbinsville was started by Fred and Ted Cobbins a few years ago while he was off fighting the war. They hadn't cared about becoming a thriving metropolis; they just wanted a nice place to live.

It was just that; a nice, quiet place to live with no real problems. He liked being a lawman here. Ted

Cobbins ran the general store, and Maude Evans ran the restaurant next door. No saloons, no drunken cowboys firing shots at the citizens, or anything like that.

And now they finally had a Church.

They had only finished the Church building last month. Most of the local families had chipped in time and labor to get it finished after they had offered Parson Stone to take the pulpit.

He had known Parson Stone since the war. They fought in the same company from '61 until the Battle for Atlanta in '64. He'd lost track of the Parson after being shot, and eventually ended up being sent home to recover.

Things had been difficult for him at home though. The war ended not long after he got back, so he tried to put it all behind him. There were too many memories of the war though, bad memories that the quiet of home didn't cover up. One day he mounted up his horse and drifted south through Colorado and New Mexico, then across through Arizona before making it back home. He had worked here and there, trying to stay busy enough so the memories could have time to fade. He'd finally found his calling after hiring on as a deputy in a little Spanish town called 'Las Placitas del Rio Bonito' in New Mexico. He always thought the name was funny, meaning something about a town by a river being pretty or some such nonsense. He'd enjoyed working there for a few years, until a 'businessman' began cheating people out of their money and land. That was about the time they finally changed the name of the place to something he could spell, Lincoln.

James sighed at the memory. He'd enjoyed enforcing the law, but since the businessman... he frowned as he tried to remember the man's name. Murphy. Lawrence Murphy.

He nodded to himself, pretty sure that was his name. Since Murphy had political connections, he was protected from the law hindering his endeavors. Not that the Sheriff of that town was too interested in hindering him, considering the kickbacks he was getting paid. He had no interest in taking bribes, so he turned in his badge, and started heading for home.

When he finally made his way home, the town offered him the job as Sheriff. It was right after that that Parson Stone had also moved to the area and ended up marrying Widow Stanton.

He topped out on a hill that overlooked the town. Sighing, he tugged the reins, and pulled the horse to a stop as he looked out over the valley.

Yeah, he was happy here now. Even in the quiet.

Movement in the distance caught his eye. He could see dust rising off the trail; probably the stage coming in.

Nudging his horse, he began moving down the hill toward town.

****

Catherine stretched as she stepped out of the stage. Her entire body ached from the long ride and cramped quarters.

"Excuse me."

She moved out of the way as the smelly businessman pushed past her and stood in the street looking around. "Where's the saloon? I need to get a drink."

"No saloon in this town mister, but we got about fifteen minutes while we change horses if you want a bite in the restaurant," The teamster spoke from the top of the stage where he was untying her trunk.

"No saloon?" The businessman whined.

Catherine struggled to remember his name, Carver or something...

"Catherine?"

She turned at the familiar voice, squealing as she recognized her sister. "Elizabeth!" She rushed forward, almost tripping on the stairs as her dress caught on the rough wood of the step.

Her sister caught her in a tight hug before stepping back, "Let me look at you! You've changed so much!"

Laughing, Catherine stepped back and curtsied, "Yep, all grown up now." Her smile faded a bit as she looked around at the town. "This place is... smaller than I thought."

Elizabeth beamed, "It's small, but it grows on you."

"Can we hurry this up?"

They looked up, the teamster had Catherine's large trunk balanced awkwardly on the edge of the coach. "Oh, I'm sorry!" Elizabeth exclaimed. "Let me get someone..." She opened the door to the store, and yelled in, "Teddy! Can you come out and help with Catherine's bags?"

Catherine stood on the edge of the boardwalk eyeing the town critically. There wasn't much to it; the building they were in front of was a front for two businesses; the store and... she leaned to the side to get a better look at the sign... a restaurant. There were a few houses on either side. Turning, she looked across the street. A solitary building stood across the street. It was a squat, ugly building that was easy to recognize by the bars over the window. It was the jail.

Further down the street was a large barn with a corral. A man was leading some horses from the barn, evidently to switch out with the stages. She wiped her face with her handkerchief; it was hot out here.

"Ah, Sheriff Matthews, it's good to see you! This is my sister, Catherine..."

Catherine turned; a man was talking with Elizabeth. He was tall. He stood a good foot higher than her 5'1" and his clothes were soaked with sweat. He smiled, taking his hat off, and bowing slightly.

"Ma'am, nice to meet you." He offered his hand.

Smiling sweetly, she stepped forward, taking his hand. He gripped hers tightly; her eyes widened at the firm grip.

"I've known your sister for a bit. Good to meet you. You gonna be here for a while?"

Catherine blinked back the tears. He needed a bath, badly. She wondered absently if all men out west smelled this bad. "Yes, for... a time." She smiled again, stepping back, "I just need to get my trunk..." she was looking for any reason to step away from this smelly... she glanced at the badge on his chest... Sheriff.

"Oh, I'll get that." He stepped forward, following her down the steps.

She hurried down, intending to grab the trunk from the teamster. She was surely strong enough; she had hauled it from the train to the stage in Laramie after all. She reached for it as the teamster started to let it down, "I've got it."

"Ma'am, it's awful heavy looking," the Sheriff warned from the side.

She gripped the handle, and started to pull it from the teamster. "No, it's not..." she broke off as she got the full weight of the trunk. She reeled backwards, fighting for balance as the heavy trunk came down hard, striking the sheriff in the side of the head as they both fell to the ground.

"Oh my goodness!" Elizabeth exclaimed from the boardwalk. "Are you all right?"

Catherine sat up, embarrassed, as she tried to get up from the ground. Her dress was covered in dust and dirt. The teamster had jumped down, apologizing profusely. As she got up, she noticed Sheriff Matthews sitting up, blood running down the side of his face.

****

Chapter Two

James sat at his desk, holding the rag to his head. He had his feet propped up on his desk, trying to get comfortable, but that was difficult with the pain shooting through his skull.

He'd been praying that the pain would stop; every bit of noise seemed to make his head throb harder. The most recent culprit was a buckboard that just rolled into town. Actually, he had been listening to it since it started down the long hill on its way into town, creaking and clattering over the rocks and bumps. He had hoped it would continue through town, but it rolled to a stop in front of the jail, and he heard the squeak of a brake being applied. There were low voices, and footsteps on the porch of the jail.

"...in his office, Doc."

James groaned, sure, he was in pain, and he could feel the large knot sticking out the side of his head through the rag, but he didn't need a doctor. Why did they call the Doc?

The door opened slowly, and Doc Merten peeked in. "James? Heard you got hurt today."

He glanced at the door and shook his head, "It's nothin' Doc. They shouldn't have wasted your time making you ride in."

Doc Merten smiled as he stepped into the room, "Nonsense, I was coming into town anyway. Caroline was running low on tea." He set his bag down on the desk and faced James. "Now, look into my eyes."

James stared ahead as the Doc leaned in close, his eyes flickering from one eye to the other. "Well, pupils are equal. That's a good sign." He straightened, "Are you feeling nauseous?"

James shook his head gently, "No Doc, just pain in the side of my head." He pulled the towel away from his head, it was covered in blood. "See."

"Piffle. Even a scratch would bleed like that. Bleeding doesn't mean you're hurt. I'm more worried about damage on the inside. Let me look."

James sat quietly while the Doc probed and prodded the lump on his skull. "Good sized goose egg, but you'll be fine; I'm sure." He smiled, "Mrs. Cobbins said you were hit with a trunk?"

14

"Yeah, her sister got into town today. Tried to pull it off the stage by herself. I was going to help..."

"Well, by the look of you, you kept it from hitting the ground and breaking." He laughed heartily at his own joke.

James smiled; it was good to see the Doc smiling again. Just a few months ago he had lost his oldest son to an accident.

"Well, James, I think you'll live." He stepped back, grinning. "Of course, we may need your services in another few weeks. My oldest, Margaret, is coming west. She just finished medical school. She will have lots of breakable things for you to save from hitting the ground." He laughed uproariously at his own joke.

James shook his head, wincing at the pain it caused. "Not doin' it that way ever again." He cocked his head slightly, "I didn't know you had another daughter."

Turning serious, Doc nodded. "She stayed east when we moved here, she wanted to go to college, then later decided on medical school." Doc pulled up a chair and sat down, facing James. "She couldn't make it for Walter's funeral. We didn't even get word to her until a few weeks after it happened. She was brokenhearted when she got the news..." He trailed off, then added softly, "But we're excited she is finally coming west."

"I'm glad for you. Let me know if there's anything I can do."

Doc grinned, "Want to help me with my bag?"

****

Catherine danced down the steps the next morning, feeling good. She had had a good night's rest with a lovely wind blowing through her window. For the first time since heading west, she felt refreshed.

She walked into the store; Elizabeth was standing behind the counter, going through their ledger. She looked up from her reading and smiled, "Good morning."

"Morning!" She walked over to the counter, "I want to help."

Elizabeth smile broadened. "Of course, that would be great. What do you want to do?"

Catherine leaned in close, giggling. "I have no clue. I've never worked in a store."

"Silly, you've probably never worked."

They shared a laugh as the little bell on the front door chimed. A tall man walked in, he was wearing a clerical collar around his neck, and was followed by a little boy.

"Parson, Thomas! Good to see you. You're out and about early."

The Parson smiled, taking off his hat. "Ladies." He stopped, and cleared his throat.

The little boy stopped, and looked at the Parson. His face suddenly turned red and he whipped his hat off, smiling apologetically, "Sorry."

"That's fine, Thomas." He turned back to Elizabeth. "Yes Ma'am, we are trying to work out some details on the social. It's coming up in a few weeks."

"We will definitely be there." She smiled, "Oh, and Parson, this is my sister, Catherine. She just got in yesterday from Philadelphia."

He nodded and offered his hand, "William Stone, it's nice to meet you, Ma'am." He gestured to the boy behind him, "And this is Thomas."

She smiled and shook his hand. He was gentle; a sharp contrast to the Sheriff who tried to break her hand shaking it yesterday. "It's nice to meet you as well, Parson Stone." She tilted her head to see around the Parson before adding, "...and Thomas."

The little boy had hung back, eyeing the candy case with hungry eyes. He glanced at her and nodded a quick greeting. Catherine laughed; it was just like a young boy to be focused on candy.

"So, what can I do for you today, Parson?" Elizabeth asked.

The Parson laughed, "Well, I promised Thomas that he could pick out two-bits worth of candy if he rode in with me today."

"Wow!" Elizabeth laughed, "Two-bits worth. That's a lot of candy, Thomas. Are you going to share?"

The boy smiled, "No Ma'am."

They all laughed at his response. Catherine happened to look down, and noticed the Parson was wearing a gun.

A gun?

She stepped back, the conversation continued to drone as the little boy pointed at different candies. Elizabeth promised to bag them as the Parson and the boy left to go talk to Sheriff Matthews.

Catherine stared, wide eyed as the Parson walked out of the store. She turned to Elizabeth, who was counting candies into a small bag. She cleared her throat. "Was that normal?"

Elizabeth answered without looking up, as she continued to count. "Was what normal, sweetie?"

"That was the Parson?"

"Uh-huh."

"As in Church?"

Elizabeth finally looked up, "Yes, that's what Parsons usually are for. Why?"

Exasperated, Catherine gestured to the door. "But, he had a gun!"

"Oh..." Shrugging, Elizabeth went back to counting. "Yeah, it is an old one too. Ted had a hard time finding ammunition for him."

"Does he always carry a gun?" Catherine was incredulous. What was wrong with people out here?

"Well, yes." She looked up, contemplative. "I think he takes it off for Church, but I could be wrong."

"Could be wro... what?" She stared, horrified at the thought of a Parson preaching a Church service wearing a gun. It was just... wrong.

Elizabeth shook her head. "Catherine, you have to remember, this isn't Philadelphia. It's dangerous out here. Criminals, Indians, and even wild animals. The Parson almost lost his life to a bear last year." She smiled, "That was right after he and his wife Anna met."

Catherine recoiled in surprise, "They met? They just got married?"

"Yes, last December." She sighed. "But really sweetie, you're going to have to get used to men carrying guns.

Catherine shook her head. "I can understand some people, but the Parson?"

"He's a really nice man." She finished counting the candy into the sack, and tied it off. "He fought in the war with James." She smiled, "You know, Sheriff Matthews. The one you hit with your trunk."

Catherine pouted; they wouldn't let her live that down, would they? "I told him I was sorry."

"And he accepted the apology, but that doesn't mean I'm not going to tease you unmercifully about it."

They shared a quiet laugh. Catherine picked up the feather duster and started dusting the shelves.

Elizabeth sighed, "This is nice, you know."

Catherine stopped, looking over, "What is?"

"Having someone to talk to."

"You have Ted."

Elizabeth laughed and shook her head. "Sweetie, one day when you get married, you'll realize having a husband is not always like having someone to talk to." She stuck out her jaw, hunched over and lowered her voice, "Honey, how long 'til supper? Where's my pants? Are we out of seed?" Straightening, she shook her head, "That's not a conversation."

The bell on the front door chimed as the door opened suddenly. Ted came in with an older man, pointing the man toward the back of the store. "Honey..." Ted pointed to the back, "Are we out of seed?"

Neither Elizabeth nor Catherine could stop laughing until well after the man left the store.

****

Walcott, WY

Carter pushed through the swinging doors to the saloon, blinking in the dim light. He moved directly to the bar, catching the barkeepers eye. "Rye." he stated simply.

He turned and scanned the tables for faces he recognized. He hadn't been to this town before that he could recall. He frowned, trying to remember its name... Walcott?

Shaking his head, he continued to scan the room. Whatever it was, at least this one had a saloon. Not like that flea trap he'd passed through yesterday. His eyes narrowed as he focused on a few men at a table in the back. Was that...

"Fifteen cents for the one, or two-bits if you want a second."

Grimacing, he turned to the bartender, reaching into his pocket and digging for a quarter. He tossed it on the counter, and tossed back the drink in one gulp. "Another."

He picked up the glass and continued looking around the room. There were a few men at a table playing poker, and another table had a man and a saloon girl in low conversation. His eyes focused on a table in the back. There were two men sitting quietly, he was pretty sure he knew one of them.

He picked up his drink and walked toward the table, his step faltering slightly as the man on the left sat his pistol on the table in an obvious threat. He smiled, it was definitely Hank.

"How are you, Hank?"

"I don't go by that name anymore. Call me Jensen," Hank growled. He looked up, recognition flickering across his face, "Carlyle?"

Carter grinned, "Call me Carter."

"Ah." Jensen kicked out a chair, "Have a seat, meet Vic."

Carter nodded to the man on the right, a redheaded man that reminded him of a weasel. "Howdy."

"Who's this guy, Jensen? Can we trust...?"

"He's alright," Jensen replied, cutting him off. "I said he's alright, so he's alright."

"Ok, Jensen." Vic replied hastily, picking up his drink.

Carter shook his head, deciding to ignore the man. He was twitchy, and people like that made him nervous. He looked back at Jensen, "Anything exciting going on?"

"Depends. What are you looking for?"

Carter grinned, "What we all want. Money."

Jensen nodded slowly, "Well, today is your lucky day. We need a third guy..."

****

Chapter Three

Fillmore, WY

Carter waved the fly away from his face as he stared across the dusty street. There were a lot of people in town today. That meant a lot of witnesses.

He blew out a breath. He needed money, but he didn't want to risk getting his neck stretched to get it.

"Are you ready?"

He turned and nodded curtly to Jensen, who was standing near the bank door. Time to get to work. He drew the pistol from his waistband as he pulled his kerchief over his face, "Let's go."

They burst through the door into the bank. There were only half a dozen or so people inside. Carter immediately moved to the right, "Everyone down on the ground and no one gets hurt!" He yelled, waving his pistol.

A woman in line screamed in fright. "Shut up!" Jensen roared, hitting her across the face with his pistol barrel. She fell to the floor, unconscious, blood pouring from her face.

"Jensen!" Carter shouted, incredulous. "What are you doing?"

Jensen turned, his pistol ready. "Get the money," He growled, and gestured toward the teller.

"We need to go faster." Vic yelled from the door. Carter could hear the shake in his voice.

Swallowing hard, Carter turned from Jensen toward the teller. The small man was standing behind the counter, his hands partially raised. Carter pulled the flour sack from his pocket and threw it through the grate. "Put all the money in the sack."

"Yyy...yes sir," The teller stammered. He looked like he would pass out any second.

Carter watched the man open the safe with shaking hands. He had to start over again twice.

"What's taking so long?" Vic whined from the door. "Someone could come any minute. I don't wanna..."

Carter turned to say something, but was cut off by Jensen. "Shut up you coward. We're about done." Jensen had been marching back and forth between the people on the floor, watching them closely.

"Hh...Here S...Sir," The teller spoke suddenly, holding the bag out to Carter.

Carter reached to take the bag, his eyes widening in disbelief as he found himself faced with a large pistol. "Drop the guns, gentlemen!" The little teller demanded, his voice suddenly full of confidence. Carter backed up slowly, "Hold on there..."

"Now!" The teller demanded.

There was a shot, followed closely by three others. Carter stared as the teller dropped his gun and fell back against the wall, blood pouring from several large wounds on his chest.

"Grab the money you fool!" Jensen yelled, "We've gotta go, now!"

Carter grabbed the moneybag from the counter where the teller had dropped it, and turned to run for the door. He watched, in horror, as Jensen fired his pistol into the back of one of the men on the floor before he turned to leave.

Everything was slow motion after that. Carter just operated on impulse, mounting his horse and riding as fast as he could behind Vic and Jensen. He was vaguely aware of gunshots behind him, and people screaming, but he was numb. He had been all for robbing the bank; his business ventures were going nowhere and he needed cash. Shooting the teller; that had even been understandable... but pistol-whipping a woman and shooting a man in the back as he lay on the ground?

They were going to hang for sure.

****

Egbert, WY

"Marshal?"

Annoyed, Deputy U.S. Marshal Lucas Sterling paused mid-bite and looked up from his plate. It was the first real food he had eaten in several days, and he had just sat down to enjoy it. "Yes?"

The telegraph operator stood a few feet away, fidgeting with his fingers. "We just got word from Fillmore." At the Marshal's blank look, he added. "Small town down the line. Anyway, there was a robbery down there, and a few people were killed."

Lucas frowned and put down his fork, "Jensen?"

"Pretty sure. The robbers wore masks." The operator paused a second, then added, "They shot one of the customers in the back while they lay on the ground."

Lucas nodded, it sounded like Jensen. He thought hard. He remembered Fillmore now; it was a good two day's ride, maybe even three, but he had no interest in riding when he could get there faster by train. "When is the next train heading there?"

"Tomorrow morning."

He closed his eyes, calculating in his head. "That'll be the quickest. Send them word I'll be there tomorrow by train."

"Yes sir."

Lucas blew out a breath in frustration. He had been tracking Jensen for the past few months. He and his crew had hit a bank in Greely, Colorado about nine weeks previous. Six people had died in the shooting, including two of Jensen's men.

He sighed and picked his fork up, taking the bite he had already cut. He had expected a lot of things when he chose to become a Deputy U.S. Marshal, but lack of good food was not on the list. In the time he had worked as a Marshal he had investigated murders, bank robberies, and train hold ups. The one thing they all had in common was that he was constantly on the move, with little time to pause and enjoy himself.

He took another bite of his steak and chewed slowly, savoring the flavor. It was not the finest steak he had eaten, and... he frowned at the dried crust of something that was on the edge of the plate, but it was definitely better than the jerky he'd been eating on the trail.

He smiled as he cut another bite. He was still young enough to remember liking jerky, back before it became his main food source.

He'd only been a U.S. Marshal for a few years, hired right after graduating from Harvard in '69. His father had sent him to school, like his older brother before him, so he could run the family business. Unfortunately, he had no interest whatsoever in managing a store. His brother was great with people; always encouraging his workers to step out and do their best.

Lucas had a difficult time seeing good in many people. He'd been six when a bank robber shot his mother in front of him. Since then, his goal was to make criminals pay for their crimes.

That had a negative impact on his relationships. He had a hard time making friends, which was one of the reasons he loved being a Marshal; he didn't have time for friends.

Taking the last bite of his steak, he chewed thoughtfully as he considered his next move. He doubted if Jensen was going to stay anywhere close to Fillmore. He was more likely to run a good distance and find a place to spend his money. His gang had got about $600 from the bank in Greely, and it had lasted what was left of his crew about six weeks as they hopped from town to town, spending wildly. He'd been one step behind Jensen for the last hundred miles as he jumped randomly from town to town spending his cash, first north of the line, then south. A few times he had even retraced his steps; returning to a town right after Lucas had left.

28

He had tried to guess Jensen's stop this time, and missed by over a hundred miles.

He wiped his face with the napkin, hoping it was cleaner than the rest of the restaurant. With the way Jensen was going through money, it would be easier to get an idea of where he might pop up next once he got an idea of how much money he took in Fillmore. Meanwhile, he was going to get to bed early and get some sleep.

****

Carter stared into the fire, watching as the flames licked at the wood, occasionally sending glowing embers into the night sky. He remembered sitting around a fire with his Pa once; it was the last memory he had of him. They were on the run after stealing a horse. It turned out the man they stole it from had been an Army Colonel. He frowned at the memory, that had been thirty odd years ago, and he could remember it clearly. He was probably six or seven... his Pa had called the glowing embers 'fireflies' that night.

They got caught the next morning, and his Pa was hanged before noon.

"I don't wanna hang," Vic offered suddenly.

Startled, Carter looked up. Vic was standing at the edge of the firelight, nervously holding his hat.

"Sit down and shut up, you fool," Jensen growled from his bedroll. He had lain down earlier, demanding that they keep watch while he got some shuteye.

Carter watched as Vic visibly wilted at the command. He came over and sat by the fire, reaching for the coffeepot and a cup. Carter shook his head; Vic's hands were still shaking. He tried to pour a cup, but was spilling more than he got into the cup.

Carter reached over and took the pot and cup from Vic, poured Vic a cup, then refilled his own. Vic smiled gratefully as he accepted the cup.

It had been a horrible day. They had ridden out of Fillmore at breakneck speed. A small posse had immediately given chase, but they had fallen behind after a few miles.

Carter had to admit, Jensen was cold, but he was a planner. The horses they had ridden into town had been stolen. He had their horses, rested and fresh, waiting for them a few miles outside of town. They had switched horses and continued riding while the posse had to slow down to keep from killing their horses.

They had ridden twenty or so miles, switching direction a few times to throw off their trail.

"Do you think we'll hang?" Vic whispered softly.

Carter shook his head slowly, "No, I think we're good."

"But he shot that man in the back!" Vic tried to whisper, but his voice rose a full octave. Nervously, he tried to take a sip of his coffee, but ended up spilling it down the front of his shirt.

Carter reached over and patted Vic's shoulder. "It came off alright. We'll be fine. Why don't you get some sleep?"

"I can't sleep..."

"It'll be fine. I'll take watch." He nodded toward Jensen, who had begun snoring in his blankets. "If he's not worried, you shouldn't be worried."

"Alright."

Vic stood and flicked the coffee from his cup. He stood for a minute staring at the flames before dropping the cup by the fire and moving over to his bedroll. He started to take off his boots, but stopped and looked over at Carter. "I might sleep with my boots on."

Carter huffed out a quiet laugh, "Safer that way. You won't have any snakes end up in your boot that way."

Vic lay down and rested his head on his saddle.

Carter sighed deeply. It was bad enough that he had his own fears of hanging, but to be forced to play nursemaid to this fool... he blew out a breath. It wasn't the glorious end to the day he had pictured. He had envisioned riding off with the money long before anyone knew the bank had been hit, and then staying the night in a hotel after they split up the money. Maybe even knocking back a few rounds of drinks beforehand.

Instead, he was out in the middle of nowhere, being hunted by a posse planning a necktie party.

He gripped his rifle tightly as he listened to Jensen snoring. It was going to be a long night.

****

Chapter Four

James woke up to the sound of birds chirping. He groaned as he opened his eyes; he hated birds. The sun wasn't even over the horizon yet, and they wouldn't let him sleep. He lay there for a few moments, thinking about staying in bed, but finally decided against it. He swung his feet off the side of the bed, blinking slowly to wake himself. He had wanted to be up early anyway. It was Saturday, and he had planned on visiting some of the locals today.

He leaned over and lit the lamp that was on the stand next to his bed, and then looked around his small room. When they gave him the job as Sheriff, they couldn't promise much in the way of pay; ten dollars a month, free meals at the restaurant, and a room in the Jail. It wasn't much, but it was better than living with Earl. Earl's cooking was almost as bad as his own.

He grinned to himself as he stood, reaching for his pants. He wanted to get by Widow Johnson's at some point today. She had a small ranch just outside of town. He needed to make sure she was coming to Church in the morning; he had been using Ted's buckboard to pick her up for services. It just happened that Saturday was the day she made cobbler. She had promised Elderberry cobbler this week.

He was fairly sure she made the cobbler to ensure he was going to visit, and he had no problem with that, but would have visited her anyway.

Grabbing his pistol belt from the desk, he slung the belt around his narrow hips, and looked over at the mirror he had hung on the wall. He took a few steps closer, and rubbed his jaw as he eyed his reflection critically.

It wasn't that he was exceptionally ugly. He smiled at that thought. Now, old Jud Pilkin, he was an ugly man. No, it wasn't that. He was a normal looking man; a tad over six feet in his socks, greenish grey eyes, brownish hair that he liked to keep short. Yep, he looked... average.

Maybe that was his problem, he was just too average. All those dandies in the dime novels were incredibly handsome with a winning smile that wooed the ladies. He smiled wide for a second, the smile fading as he noticed his missing lower tooth. He had lost it while biting down on his knife handle when they were cutting a bullet out of his leg.

He shook his head at the memory. That hadn't been his brightest decision, but it was better than losing the leg to the saw.

The point was, he wasn't going to woo too many ladies looking like this; that was for certain.

He turned from the mirror and grabbed his hat off the hook. He'd have to worry about wooing the ladies later. Right now he needed to get moving

****

"Here you go, dearie, Elderberry cobbler." Widow Johnson put the plate with the steaming piece of cobbler on the table in front of him.

"Oh, Mrs. Johnson, you shouldn't have!" James grinned as he picked up his fork.

"Nonsense, dearie. I made that special for you." She poured him a cup of coffee, then sat across from him watching him eat. "I just worry about you, dearie. You're going to wither away. I might not be here too much longer to take care of you."

"Mrs. Johnson!"

"No, no…" She raised her hand, "I don't want to hear all of that. I know I'm getting on in years." She shook her head. "I just think you need a wife."

James choked on his cobbler. "Mrs. Johnson!" He sputtered between coughs. "I mean, I really respect you..."

"Oh, now!" She slapped his arm, "I don't mean me."

Relieved, James sat back and took a sip of his coffee.

"Parson and Anna were over yesterday. They seem real happy." Widow Johnson frowned, "You should have married her."

James started choking on his coffee, and started to speak, but she held up her hand again.

"Now, I know the Good Lord put them two together, so that's alright. Let bygones be bygones I always say."

Staring wide eyed, James took another sip of his coffee. This was the weirdest visit he had ever had with Widow Johnson.

"We still need to find you a wife. Anna mentioned there was a new girl in town. You better snatch her up before someone else does."

James could only stare as she talked. He opened his mouth, "I... uh..."

She gestured to his plate, "Finish your cobbler, dearie. It's getting cold."

****

As James rode away from Widow Johnson's house, he was convinced that he didn't need cobbler that bad anymore.

He rode a long route around the town, checking on some of the other locals. He was technically out of his jurisdiction; his 'official' duties ended at the Cobbinsville town limits, but he liked being there for others if they needed him.

James topped out on a hill, a long valley stretched out below him shimmering in the summer heat. Taking off his hat, he wiped his face with the back of his hand and put his hat back on. He could hear the distant roll of thunder as clouds piled in the southwest. There was a storm rolling in, probably later that day. He rode down the hill at a slow trot, not really in a hurry, but wanting to feel the wind on his face. He liked to ride. Having the wind in his face was more comfortable than swatting flies in his office. He was looking forward to winter. At least there would be fewer bugs.

He stopped by three more ranches before heading back toward town. It was getting late in the day, and he was starting to get a tad saddle sore.

By the time James reached town, there was a cool breeze following him. He looked behind him, his brow furrowing as he considered the line of clouds that had effectively overtaken the sky. It definitely wasn't going to be a gentle shower; that was for sure.

****

Catherine stepped out onto the store's porch, inhaling deeply. The wind was cool as it blew through town. She could smell the fresh scent of pines on the breeze. Walking across the porch, she sat on the porch swing and closed her eyes as she relaxed in the cool breeze. It was still hot in the store, even with the windows open.

She could hear thunder off in the distance. It sounded like it was coming from the west. Leaning forward, she looked up the road toward the setting sun. It was just disappearing over the hill, but she could see dark clouds surrounding it.

She sat back and smiled to herself. She was looking forward to some rain. It would probably cut down some of this infernal dust that continually hung in the air. She closed her eyes, and relaxed. It felt good to just sit here and not do anything. It seemed like she had been constantly busy since she arrived, so sitting felt good.

The sound of a horse coming up the street tore her from her reverie. She opened her eyes, looking to the left. The Sheriff was riding up the narrow street. He had noticed her on the porch, and had angled his horse toward the store. Her hands lifted automatically to her hair as several thoughts ran through her mind. First, she wondered how badly she looked after being in the hot store all day long. She also wondered if she should apologize again for hitting him with her trunk.

The Sheriff pulled up a few feet from the porch and took off his hat. "Howdy, ma'am. Sure is cooling off."

She smiled widely, "It is. How are you doing Sheriff Matthews? Out chasing criminals?"

He laughed, "No Ma'am, there ain't enough criminals around here to keep me very busy. I was visiting some of the surrounding ranches and farms."

She recoiled in surprise, "Really?"

"Yes Ma'am." He looked puzzled, "Does that surprise you?"

"Well..." She started, her brow furrowed. "Living in Philadelphia, we have police for just the city. They don't go out." She shrugged apologetically, "I guess there are a lot of differences."

"Yes Ma'am... Well, my authority only extends to the edge of town, but we try to make everyone feel like they are part of the community." He paused as a roll of thunder crashed a little closer. He glanced up at the sky, then asked, "Speaking of which, how are you liking Cobbinsville?"

"That depends, Sheriff; do you want the honest truth, or the nice things you are supposed to tell people?"

He grinned widely, "Ma'am, call me James. Sheriff Matthews is a mouthful, and I guess it's all up to you which story you spin."

Laughing, she shook her head. "Really, James, I like it here. The size takes some getting used to."

"Yes Ma'am," He offered in mock seriousness, "It is pretty big at that. Makes people scared of getting lost."

"There is that." She brushed at the sleeve of her dress, noting the small cloud of dust that came off. "But the dust is horrible out here..." She was cut off by a loud roll of thunder that seemed to shake the building.

James was looking up at the sky, concern etched on his face. "Well, Ma'am..."

"Call me Catherine."

"Catherine," He reddened slightly, to her amusement. "I'll tell you what; I'm glad you're settlin' in and gettin' used to the place, and I'd love to talk more, but there's a storm coming. My brother likes to call these 'gulley washers.' That'll take care of the dust for a few days." As if to prove his point, a few large drops of rain fell, each sending up a little puff of dust.

Surprised, she leaned forward. In the time they had been talking the clouds had completely covered the sky. It was getting dark quickly.

"Ma'am, I think you may want to get inside before this one hits. I need to get my horse put up."

She stood, "Thank you, James. Be safe."

"Yes Ma'am." He rode off quickly down toward the livery.

She watched him until he reached the building, then smiling; she went back into the store.

****

Catherine stared at the ceiling as it was lit up by the flashes of lightning. She had hoped that a good storm would help her sleep, but there was no way that was happening tonight. Every time the thunder sounded it shook the entire house on its frame and rattled the windows. She was half afraid that they would break from the shaking.

She had never been scared before during a storm. Her parents' house in Philadelphia was a large stone house that was so solid she hardly knew when there was a storm.

She huffed out a laugh as she rolled over on her side. There was no chance of that here. Right before she went to bed it had started hailing; huge chunks of ice the size of quarters. They sounded like gunshots as they hit the roof, and it had sent her scurrying for cover. She didn't think Ted would ever stop laughing. Alfred would have...

She felt her face tighten. She hated thinking about Alfred. He'd made her care for him, and then made her look like a fool for doing it.

She rolled onto her side and faced the wall, staring at the pattern on the wood planks with each lightning strike. There was a large knot in the wood that looked like that portrait of Great Aunt Belinda that hung in her parent's hall. Alfred had always said...

She frowned, annoyed. She couldn't get through a night without thinking about him. That was why she had come west to begin with. She had hoped she could find something to keep her mind off of him. When you've spent two years of your life caring for someone, two years hoping they would be a permanent part of your life, their memories tended to touch every aspect of your life. Everything seemed to spark a memory that you shared with that person. Even packing her trunk to come west had triggered memories, since Alfred had been with her the day her father had bought them for her trip to Baltimore. He had even carried them to the train that day so she wouldn't drop it...

Like she had on the Sheriff's head.

The sudden shift in thought brought a thin smile to her face. The Sheriff... James, she corrected herself, seemed like a nice man. She hadn't liked him much when they first met. Her smile widened as she recalled how badly he had smelled. He hadn't seemed like someone with much depth, but finding out that he spent his time checking on the people outside of town, time he didn't have to use... Ted had nothing but good things to say about him. He said the town could hardly afford to pay him, but he took his job seriously, and was a hard worker.

She blinked slowly as the lightning slowly died out. The gentle thrum of the rain was comforting as she grew tired. James was a nice man. She just wished that Alfred had been more like James; if he had been, she could have been happy.

The rain continued to fall long after she drifted off to sleep.

****

Chapter Five

Anna grabbed the edge of the seat as the buckboard rocked violently over another bump. They had been on the trail for an hour already, and had a long way to go.

"Sorry," William offered from the seat next to her. "Bumpy road."

She smiled and patted his arm. "Its fine, William."

"Well, I don't want anything to..."

She laughed, "Oh William, stop worrying. I'm expecting, not dying."

He flashed a grin, and then turned to focus on the trail.

She sighed softly, shifting slightly in her seat. It was a long ride into town, several hours in the buckboard as a matter of fact, and it was a trip she just wasn't used to. Since Clay died, she had rarely left the house, and never came into town, but since marrying William and building the Church this past spring she had taken the long journey to town every week.

Now, since she was expecting, the journey was getting even more trying. The further along she got the more uncomfortable the ride was.

Smiling to herself, she leaned her head on William's shoulder as he drove the cart. Things had changed so much for her this past year. She had met William when he stopped at her ranch looking for work. They fell in love, despite... She pulled her scarf closer over the side of her face. He had seen past her looks and loved her for who she was.

She had to admit, it was a switch suddenly being the Parson's wife. She had hidden from people for years, but now was put in the limelight. She was still a tad sensitive when it came to the burn scars on her face...

"Ma, can I sit with Mr. James during the service today?" Thomas asked suddenly from the rear of the buckboard, interrupting her reverie.

She lifted her head and turned to look back, but a wave of nausea washed over her. She swallowed hard and gritted her teeth until the feeling passed, then answered. "That is entirely up to James. You were a little fidgety last week."

"Well, Mr.... Parson William talked a real long time last week."

William laughed aloud, "Well, I guess you're right about that. I almost put myself to sleep up there." He glanced over his shoulder. "But, Church ain't too safe of a place to sleep, is it?"

Thomas giggled, "No sir, not if you're sitting in a window."

Anna relaxed as she listened to their light banter. William and Thomas had just had a long discussion yesterday over dinner about a young man named Eutychus, who fell asleep while the Apostle Paul was preaching. He fell out of a window and died, but was brought back to life—It was a good story to warn others about sleeping in Church.

"You know..." William had turned serious, "Sometimes the things in the Bible aren't very exciting. That was why Eutychus fell asleep. But they are things that need to be said. And if they need to be said...?"

"They need to be listened to?" Thomas offered.

"Exactly."

Anna lay her head back on William's shoulder and smiled in satisfaction. One of the first things she had grown to love about William was how he treated Thomas. Even though he was only ten, William took the time to listen to him and talk with him about things; often turning their talks into life lessons that Thomas needed. Not many men would take the time to make a boy feel important, but William had.

"But, last week you was preaching..."

"Were preaching..." Anna interrupted softly.

"Yes ma'am, were preaching on giving. It didn't seem like many people wanted to hear about that."

"Well, that's true." William laughed loudly, which cut off as the buckboard hit another bump, causing Anna to jostle against William's shoulder. He looked down at her, "Sorry."

Anna looked up into his eyes; she loved looking into his blue eyes. "Its fine William, stop apologizing." She knew if she didn't say something he was going to keep doing it, and that would be the conversation for their entire trip.

William grinned and looked back at the trail. "Well, Thomas, it's important to listen to sermons you don't want to hear, because those are the ones you really need."

"Yes sir." Thomas fell silent for a few seconds, and then asked, "So, can I sit with Mr. James?"

****

Catherine woke up late on Sunday. She jumped out of bed, anxious to get ready for Church. It was going to be her first service in Cobbinsville, and she didn't want to be late.

She pulled one of her dresses from the narrow closet. It was one of her more simple ones, blue with narrow sleeves. She had seen what Elizabeth was wearing, and didn't want to make her feel frumpy. She huffed out a laugh; she probably wouldn't need half of the dresses she had packed.

She held the dress in front of her as she looked in the mirror; the color of the dress brought out the blue in her eyes.

Perfect.

She dressed quickly, despite the narrowness of her room. She remembered looking at it skeptically when Elizabeth had brought her upstairs. She had a closet back in Philadelphia that was just as big. Not wanting to hurt Elizabeth's feelings, she had gushed about how cozy it was.

Finishing, she looked critically at her hair in the mirror. She had parted it down the center with a braid in the back. There wasn't much else she could do with her hair when it was going to fall flat anyway because of the heat. She was starting to see why many women wore the style bonnets that they did. She pinned on her hat, sighed and decided it would be good enough.

She raced down the narrow steps to the main room. Elizabeth was already waiting for her, smiling as she looked her over. "You look beautiful, Catherine. Teddy already walked over to the Church to talk with the men, so it's just the two of us."

"Oh, Ok." Catherine smiled, "I'm ready."

****

Catherine walked up the brief set of stairs and stepped through the door to the Church, immediately surprised at the number of people that were there. She didn't think there were this many people in town! "Where did all these people come from?" She whispered to Elizabeth.

Elizabeth leaned over, "Most of these people traveled a long way to get here."

"Really?" She looked around the building. The Church was small, really not much larger than the store. There were two rows of benches, with a narrow aisle down the middle. She counted at least twenty people already in the building, and she had passed several others on the way in.

They had barely made it through the door when they were stopped by a smiling woman. "Oh, Elizabeth, is this your sister?"

Catherine smiled at the woman. She was wearing a pretty yellow dress, one that would have been fairly plain in Philadelphia, but seemed almost elegant for Cobbinsville.

"Oh, yes. Catherine, this is Caroline, the Doctor's wife. Caroline, my little sister, Catherine."

Catherine took the hand that Caroline offered and smiled sweetly, "Pleased to meet you."

Caroline beamed in delight, "You as well, welcome to town." She looked behind them, "Oh, look, here comes the Parson. We'll talk after the service."

They quickly moved forward and took a seat on the fifth row. It was already starting to warm up, even with the windows open, so Catherine pulled out her fan and started waving it as they waited for the Parson to come in.

A young boy; she smiled as she recalled meeting Thomas, the Parson's stepson, came in carrying a huge case. Catherine nodded appreciatively; she recognized a Cello case. She had a friend back East who played the Cello, and she loved the sound. He carried it to the front, to a little alcove to the right of the pulpit where a piano sat, and sat it gently on the floor next to a chair.

The Parson came in, closely followed by a woman in an older style green dress wearing a scarf over her hair. She followed him to the platform, and then moved to the right where Thomas had placed the Cello.

The Parson stepped behind the pulpit, "Let us stand and sing, 'Shall we gather at the river' together."

Catherine was surprised that the piano remained untouched during the singing. Instead, they were accompanied by the Cello.

After the hymn ended, she leaned over to her sister and whispered, "Who is that on the Cello? She plays wonderfully."

Elizabeth whispered back, "That is Anna... Mrs. Stone, the Parson's wife."

Catherine nodded to herself. It now made sense why young Thomas was carrying the Cello to the front. She watched her as she played through the next hymn. She played with a passion that was evident.

They went through several other hymns before the plate was passed. Catherine was surprised by the number of people who seemed to give willingly. She smiled, thinking they must love their Parson and their Church.

After the offering, the Parson stood back at the front. "Turn in your Bibles to the Gospel of Matthew, Chapter 7."

There was the rustling of pages as everyone turned to the passage. Catherine turned to the page quickly, and then looked around while others were finding their place. Most of the people in attendance looked solemn and attentive.

She noticed Thomas had taken a place sitting by James on the third row. Curious, she looked back at the front. Mrs. Stone was still in her place on the far side of the platform with her Bible in her lap. She wondered if James was related to them.

"Stand if you will, for the reading of God's Word..." The Parson spoke quietly, "I just want to read one verse in your hearing, verse 21. *'Not every one that saith unto me, Lord, Lord, shall enter into the kingdom of heaven...'"* He paused and looked at the congregation. "Just because you say you know Christ, that doesn't mean that he knows you. Let's bow our heads in prayer."

He led the Church in a short prayer, and had them sit down as he started speaking earnestly about Salvation. Catherine tried to listen to the service, but found that watching the other people's reaction much more intriguing. There was a mixture of reactions from the small congregation. Many of them had an interested look as they watched the Parson speak, there were a few that seemed to hang on his every word with rapt attention.

Then there were the ones who watched with haughty indifference. There was even one large woman who took every opportunity to roll her eyes; making a show of letting the Parson see her reaction.

Catherine shook her head. It was sad that people like that came to Church, since their goal seemed to be to ruin it for others. She knew she was a Christian. She had accepted Christ when she was a little girl, and never got tired of hearing messages about it.

The Parson finished the message, explaining to them that Heaven was a gift that God wanted to give them, with an invitation to accept Christ as their Savior. Mrs. Stone began playing *'Just As I Am'* on the Cello as the Parson extended the invitation to come forward and pray.

****

Catherine moved through the crowd, making straight for Mrs. Stone. She was sitting in her chair, packing the Cello back in its case, and didn't notice Catherine until she stood next to her. "Mrs. Stone?"

Startled, Mrs. Stone looked up; Catherine could see a hesitant smile behind the scarf that covered most of her face. Elizabeth had told her that she had been burnt in the fire that killed her first husband, and that was why she wore the scarf.

"Yes? Oh, you're Elizabeth's sister, aren't you?" She stood, offering her hand, "I have been looking forward to meeting you." She laughed softly, "My Thomas told me you were pretty."

"He's a sweet boy, and I've wanted to meet you as well. Elizabeth tells me how much of a blessing you are to her."

"That's what we are supposed to do, is bless each other." She paused for a second, then added, "And please, call me Anna. I'm not that much older than you. Mrs. Stone makes me feel old."

"Alright, Anna." Catherine giggled, "I wouldn't want you to feel old."

Anna smiled and gestured to the Church, "What did you think of the service today?"

Catherine laughed, gesturing to the Cello case. "I was just coming up here to tell you how beautifully you played. I've never heard one used for hymns before. It seemed like it would be difficult to play through those." She sighed, "But you made it look easy."

"Thank you, Catherine. That means a lot."

Catherine gestured to the piano, "Why don't you play the piano though?"

Anna laughed, "No one in town can play a piano, especially me."

Confused, Catherine shrugged and wrinkled her nose, "Then why do you have one?"

Chuckling still, Anna leaned forward. "Well, a man came through last month; he was heading west to start a saloon. He had stopped in for supplies, and ran into William..." She paused at Catherine's blank look, "The Parson," she explained.

"Oh."

"Well," Anna continued, "After talking to William, the man started feeling bad. He told William he had run out on his wife and children, and left them back in Tennessee to chase his dream. By the end of the conversation he had sold his wagon, donated the piano to the Church, and was heading back to Tennessee to apologize to his wife in the hopes she would take him back." She laughed, "We haven't heard from him since, but hope it all worked out."

Catherine laughed, "Wow, that's..." She trailed off, unsure how to label that story.

"Funny is the word I use." Anna laughed again. "Meanwhile, we have a piano, but no player."

"Well," Catherine shrugged, "I play piano. I would love to accompany you sometime."

Anna's face lit up in surprise, "Really! That would be great. I'll tell William, that is an answer to prayer."

"I'm not very good though," She spoke hurriedly, not wanting Anna to get too excited. "I wouldn't feel comfortable playing by myself."

"Oh no, that is fine." She looked over Catherine's shoulder, "Oh, I'm sorry, William seems to need me. Let's plan to talk later."

Catherine nodded, "Of course." She smiled as Anna walked away; glad she had taken the time to speak to her.

****

Chapter Six

The fly moved in quick bursts across the counter. Catherine watched it with disinterest as it moved closer to the edge.

This was boring.

She dabbed her face with her handkerchief, the sudden movement startling the fly. It buzzed off to another part of the store.

Great. Now she lost her entertainment.

She didn't know what she had expected when she came west. Grand parties? Crowds of people gathering daily to discuss fashion? She sighed, closing her eyes. Even the dime novels she had read had made it exciting; a gunfight on the street every day. Indian attacks and hordes of locusts.

That may be happening somewhere, but not in this town.

She snorted derisively; she wasn't even sure she could call this a town. A Church, a store, a jail, and a restaurant. How exciting. She looked out the window, grimacing at the empty street.

Closing her eyes she thought about life back in Philadelphia. Her friends had been aghast when she announced her decision to come west.

Of course, she had to... she couldn't stay with Alfred embarrassing her like that.

She had met Alfred two years ago at a friend's party, and he was so exciting. He was so polite and kind, and had been on so many exciting adventures; most of which had been a lie, as she later found out. He was a two-bit shyster that had fooled her with his slick words. She huffed out a derisive laugh; he had fooled her, fooled her friends, and even fooled her parents.

He had been thrown in jail after being caught stealing from the bank he worked for. Embezzling money, they had called it. She had sent word to him that their engagement was off, and to not bother her again. However, she still felt the shame; everyone in town was talking about it, and whispering about her as she passed by. Then there was...

The bell on the front door chimed, interrupting her memories, as an older man shuffled through the front door. He smiled and pulled his hat from his head. "Howdy, Ma'am."

She smiled broadly, "Good afternoon, sir. May I help you?"

"Sure. I need a pound of coffee and a pound of sugar."

"Coming right up."

He grunted, and moved slowly over to the counter. "You're new."

She flashed a quick smile over her shoulder as she measured out the sugar, "My name is Catherine. I'm Elizabeth's sister."

"Huh. That's nice." He was quiet for a moment, and then asked, "Are you married?"

Catherine stiffened slightly, not another suitor! "No sir, I am not."

He grunted again, and was silent until she finished getting his coffee, and then finally spoke. "Can you get me another pound of coffee? And maybe deliver it to the jail?"

"Sure." She looked at him closely, "To a prisoner?"

He grunted out a laugh, "No, to the Sheriff. He's kin, and looked like he needed coffee. I got things to do though."

"Oh, that's fine." She shrugged, wondering what he had to do that he couldn't walk across the street, but fresh air would be nice. She wondered how they were related. He was old, probably his father. She could see a slight resemblance. "That's .32 cents. And I should tell him this is from...?"

"Earl." He pulled out two quarters, and placed them on the counter.

She got his change from the money box, and watched him leave. Sighing, she pulled off her apron and hollered, "Ted. I need to go across the street."

****

Catherine entered the jail, surprised at how nice it was. From the outside it looked like a squat, ugly building, but it wasn't bad when you first walked in. The Sheriff had an office set up at the front, with a large desk.

James jumped to his feet when she walked in. He had been sitting at his desk with his feet propped up, reading. "Ma'am."

She smiled apologetically, "Please, don't get up. I'm so sorry to bother you." She held out the bag, "I was just delivering some coffee for you. Your father sent it over."

He paused in the midst of reaching for the coffee, obviously confused. "My father?"

"Y...yes?" She wondered what kind of relationship they had. Was that why he wouldn't deliver it himself? "His name was Earl."

60

James laughed loudly, and shook his head. He took the coffee from her and threw the bag on his desk. "That scoundrel, did he tell you he was my father?"

Catherine frowned, trying to remember. "Well, not exactly... he said you were kin."

James wiped his eyes, still smiling. "Earl is my brother."

She clapped her hand over her mouth. "I'm so sorry! I didn't..."

"It's fine. I just got worried the resurrection happened all the sudden, and the dead had rose from the grave like Parson just preached on." He gestured to a chair, "Have a seat."

"Oh, no. I couldn't take up your time; you were busy when I barged in..." She trailed off as she looked down at the desk; it had several books on it. As she looked closer, she noticed most of them were reading primers. Catherine looked up, surprised. "Yours?"

"Yes Ma'am."

"Can't you read?"

James recoiled, obviously surprised by the question. "Yes ma'am..." He trailed off, and then added, "Though not real well. We didn't have a school when I was coming up. Ma died of scarlet fever when I was four. It was just me and Pa until Earl came back."

She reddened, "And Earl is your brother."

"Yes ma'am. Same Pa. His Ma died early on. He was out west mining when Pa married my Ma."

"Oh."

He shrugged, "Pa taught me a few letters, but he died when I was eleven." He paused, wrinkling his nose as he thought. "No, I was ten." Shaking his head, he continued, "It don't matter. Anyway, I got by fine until I went to war. Parson taught me how to read."

"Parson... Stone?" She nodded, remembering. "That's right, Elizabeth said you fought together."

Grinning, James nodded. "Yep. Matter of fact, he taught a few of us to read."

"So, this is just practice?"

"Yes Ma'am. I'm trying to get better, but it's slow." His face turned serious, "This is a small town, not a whole lot of people, but one day... one day we hope to grow. They'll need more than an ignorant Sheriff that can handle a gun." He gestured to the large book on the corner of his desk. "That's my goal, to read well enough to understand all of that."

She looked down at the book, 'Commentaries on the Laws of England' by Blackstone. "That is very deep reading there."

"Yes Ma'am, but that is what I need to know if I want to serve this town." He shrugged, "Every man ought to know how to read anyhow."

Catherine nodded. "That's very true." She looked back up at him; he was still flushed from embarrassment. "Sheriff, if there is anything I can do to help, let me know. It is very honorable what you want to do."

He smiled gratefully, "Yes Ma'am. Thank you, Ma'am."

As she crossed the street to go back to the store, all she could think about was how embarrassed he had been when she pointed out that he couldn't read.

****

Chapter Seven

James dismounted stiffly and led his horse across the yard. He grimaced, wondering if he was getting too old for riding around.

Of course, he was only about half Earl's age, and that old codger seemed to get around all right. He shook his head, and hollered, "Hello in the house!"

The door opened a few seconds later, Earl stuck his head out. "Well, it's 'bout time you showed up to visit. Sit a spell."

"Let me get my horse put up." He led his sorrel over to the corral and stripped the saddle and bridle before turning her loose. By the time he got back to the porch, Earl was rocking easily in one of the chairs, two cups in his hands.

"Coffee?"

"Sure." James took the offered cup and sat on the other chair, looking out over the valley. "Sometimes I miss the view from here. Not enough trees around town."

Earl grunted, "Too much dust."

They sat in silence for a while, listening to the birds chirping in the trees.

"So," Earl broke the silence, "Did you get yer coffee from the store?"

James looked over, Earl was grinning widely, obviously satisfied with himself. "Old coot, why'd you go and do that. You confused that poor girl. She thought you were my Pa."

Earl sat up straight, "Pa!"

"Yup. She said some geezer came in and ordered coffee for his young 'un across the street. She said he was too feeble to climb the steps to deliver it hisself." James hurriedly sipped his coffee to hide his smile.

"She did not." Earl frowned, "You're funnin' me."

James only held out a moment longer before bursting out laughing. "No, but she did think you was my Pa."

"Well, that's 'cause you're all wet behind the ears still."

"So, why'd you do it?"

"I didn't see you over there talkin' to her."

"What?" James looked over, surprised. "I've talked to her."

"'bout what? The weather?"

James flushed red, "Well, last week we did talk about the weather." He paused, and then added defensively. "But, I said 'Hi' to her at Church too."

"Uh-huh. That's why you need help." Earl shook his head. "Happiest day of my life was when I married my Martha. If it weren't for her..." he shook his head. "You've been alone too long, boy."

"So you want to push some gal into talking to me in the hopes that I marry her?"

Earl shrugged, and sipped his coffee before responding. "Can't hurt."

James stared down at his coffee, swirling it around in the cup for a few seconds before responding. "What makes everyone think I want to get hitched?"

Earl chuckled loudly, "What makes you think we care?"

James shook his head, then took another sip of his coffee. "Earl, you just might ask someone before planning their life. Fact is, I ain't ready to be hitched."

"Sure you are."

Frustrated, James tossed the rest of his coffee from his cup. "What do I have to offer?"

Earl stared at him for a moment. "Well, yer right. I got the looks."

"That's not what I meant." He sat back and watched Earl's dog, Honey, as she chased her tail in circles. "I'm serious, Earl. I ain't got nothin' to offer a gal. Ten dollars a month and a bed at the jail?"

"You got half this ranch too. All of it afore long, since me and Martha never had young'uns."

"Don't talk like that."

Earl grunted, "It's true. I'm getting' a tad long in the tooth to be running this too much longer."

James frowned, looking down at his cup. "That why you're in such an all-fired hurry for me to get hitched?"

Earl was silent for a few moments, and then pointed across the field, "Company comin'."

James looked up. Young Thomas was coming across the field. He shook his head and stood, looking down at Earl. "Guess we'll talk later?"

****

Catherine sighed as she looked up from her book. "I'm bored." She wasn't really fond of reading to begin with, but since this was the only thing to do...

Elizabeth looked over, "Welcome to Cobbinsville, sweetie." She chuckled softly, "When Teddy first opened the store, he had hoped the town would grow faster, but with the railroad so far north of us..." She gestured out the front window at the dusty street. "You see it's not happening very fast." She looked back down at her catalogue, "So, we wait."

"It doesn't seem like you'd make enough to live on."

Elizabeth shrugged without looking up. "We get by. We have several ranchers in the area that come for supplies on a regular basis, plus some extra sales from passengers on the stage."

"Humph." Catherine looked out the window; they were expecting the stage any time now. It used to come at two o'clock or so, but had been running an hour late this whole week. Shaking her head, she looked down at the counter and traced a circle in the dust. "Oh, look. Time to dust again."

"There you go, sweetie. Something to do."

Rolling her eyes, Catherine picked up the feather duster and began swiping at things around the store. It was pretty well dusty all the time, except right after a rain. Those hadn't come too frequently in the past few weeks.

She didn't want to be whiny; though she was sure Elizabeth thought so. She had just pictured life here a lot different from reading Elizabeth's letters.

She had to admit, it wasn't all bad. She had been enjoying herself at Church. This past Sunday had been spectacular. She had played the piano during singing to accompany Anna on her Cello, and everyone seemed to enjoy it.

She had almost froze in embarrassment when she'd hit a wrong key. She'd looked over at Anna, expecting reproof, but she had remained focused on the Cello. The Parson had just smiled, nodded, and kept singing. She'd expected to get griped at after Church, and had fretted all during the sermon—she hadn't even heard what he preached on because of her fear. But afterward everyone had simple smiled and thanked her; the Parson had even asked her to play this Saturday at the Church social.

She frowned as she remembered how Alfred would belittle her every time she made a mistake. He would tell her how pathetic of a...

"There's the stage," Elizabeth announced suddenly. "Coming over the hill."

Catherine listened intently; she could hear the faint sounds of hooves and chains. "I hear it."

"Better go next door and warn Maude."

Catherine nodded, putting the feather duster under the counter on her way out the door.

****

There was a rapid knock on the door, "Sheriff?"

James looked up from his Bible. He hadn't been back in town long, and was resting from the long ride, taking an opportunity to read. He'd heard the stage come in to town, but was trying to finish the chapter he was in. He sighed, wondering who needed him now. "Come in."

The door swung open and Ray, one of the teamsters that drove the stage, poked his head through the door, "Hey Sheriff, got a minute?"

Standing, James motioned for him to come in, "Set a spell."

"Can't, gotta get moving as soon as the horses are changed. I just wanted you to know, Hank Jensen's back in the area. Robbed a bank up in Fillmore a few days ago. Teller was shot and killed."

James shook his head, "That's bad. He'll hang for sure when they catch him."

"Yeah, likely will. I just thought you'd want to warn your people."

James nodded, "I will, thanks, Ray."

Ray closed the door behind him as he left. James stood behind his desk, looking down at the Bible. The story was just getting good too. He was reading about a man named Barak who was leading a fight against... well, it was some other strange name, but he'd have to finish it later.

He grabbed his gun belt from the hook, and buckled it around his hips. He figured he ought to go talk to Ted at the store, and Maude at the restaurant to keep an eye out.

Most of the time things were fairly peaceful here; they were so far out of the way that most criminals didn't bother passing through. When they did they didn't stay long. Having no saloon to drink at was a pretty fair invitation for them to move on down the road, but coupled with a barely surviving store and a restaurant that served what could only be described as 'passable' food... there just wasn't much to encourage wayward souls to stay.

Not that they shouldn't keep vigilant, of course. The last thing he intended was to be complacent.

He stepped out into the sun; the dust from the stage was still a low cloud over the town. There wasn't much of a breeze to clear it off. He breathed through his nose as he ran across the street, crossing in front of the stage. Ray already had the new team hitched and was getting ready to move out.

He took the stairs two at a time, and had just reached for the door handle when he heard a voice from across the street.

"Sheriff!"

He stopped and turned to see who it was.

****

Catherine had gotten used to the general tone of stage gossip after the last few weeks behind the counter. She normally heard about the latest Indian uprising, or who the fastest gunfighter was, or one of the other juicy tidbits. Today seemed similar; all the talk was about some man named Jensen, and a bank hold up. She had pretty well decided to ignore it, until she noticed Elizabeth's reaction; she was white as a sheet, and looking concerned.

Catherine stepped over, whispering, "What's wrong?"

Elizabeth looked over at her, "Have you heard them talking?"

Catherine nodded, "Yes, but..."

"Fillmore's less than fifty miles away, and Jensen is dangerous. Someone should probably tell the Sheriff."

Catherine nodded, "You want me to go get him?"

Elizabeth nodded gratefully, "Would you, sweetie? And hurry, before the stage leaves."

Catherine hurried to the door and opened it quickly, recoiling as it slammed into something on the other side. Startled, she stepped back, "Hello?"

The only response she received was loud laughter from the stagecoach. She tried to open the door again, and it swung out freely. The big teamster, Ray, was on top of the stage, doubled over with laughter. She looked around, trying to see what he found so humorous, when suddenly Sheriff James sat up from the ground in front of the stage. She stared quizzically, wondering why he was on the ground, when suddenly she understood.

She had hit him with the door.

****

James frowned as he looked in the mirror. His eye was swollen and bruising rapidly. He shook his head, "You have got to be joshin' me."

"I think it adds character," Parson Stone mused from across the room. He had his feet up on James' desk. He had been struggling to hold off his laughter.

"I look like a little kid that's been scrappin' on the playground."

"Well, sure. But it could be worse. Folks will think twice about messing with a mean looking sheriff." He chuckled softly, "Besides, you should've seen yourself reeling off the porch backwards."

"Thanks."

"No problem. That's what I'm here for. To make sure the devil doesn't take you down with pride."

"Humph." He gingerly probed his eye. "I swear that girl has it in for me."

"Oh, now." The Parson laughed softly, "She's a nice girl. Wouldn't hurt a fly."

James turned and gave the Parson a measured look.

"It was an accident, James."

"Yeah, Parson, I know." He leaned against the wall, staring out the front window of the jail. "It was just unexpected is all."

"Well, I hope that it doesn't stop you from being friendly."

"I've been friendly," He protested.

"Just keep it up then." The Parson stood, "Well, the reason I hollered was to see if you wanted to grab dinner over at Maude's. We need to talk about the social on Saturday."

"Sure." James sighed and grabbed his hat off the peg. "I guess they already seen me anyway."

****

"So, what do I do if someone comes in to rob the store?"

Ted turned sharply, "What makes you think that's a possibility?"

Catherine shrugged, "I heard you and Sheriff Matthews talking earlier, after... well, after I hit him with the door. He said something about the Jensen gang 'on the move' and all of that. After listening to the people on the stage, I just thought I should be prepared."

Ted nodded thoughtfully, "If that happens, I have a gun under the counter..."

"Teddy!"

Elizabeth's voice called from the restaurant next door, interrupting him.

"Coming." he yelled, and then turned to Catherine. "Can you watch the store for a minute?"

She smiled wide, "Sure."

She moved behind the counter as Ted left. It's not like they were in danger of getting any more customers than they had. The stage was gone, and it was just Etta Mae in the back of the store looking through the new bolts of fabric they had just got in. Other than her, the store was empty, and likely to remain so.

She didn't know what she would do if robbers came in. The dime novels always made them sound so... daring. They were always chivalrous to the ladies and polite. But she knew that was just books. What had they said about this Jensen guy? He 'pistol whipped' a woman in the face.

Whatever that was, it didn't sound chivalrous.

What had Ted told her? There was a gun under the counter? She stooped down, looking under the shelves. There! She could see a pistol in a holster by the cash box. She looked around the store. Etta was still at the fabric.

She shrugged and pulled the pistol from under the counter, hefting it in her hand. It wasn't really large. She had seen the one Sheriff Matthews carried, his was a lot bigger. She slid the leather loop off of the hammer, and pulled the little pistol from its holster.

"I could shoot this," She stated confidently. She gripped the pistol tight in her fist, and pointed it at the front door. "No, you can't have the money!"

She smiled, feeling dangerous. She pointed it at the wall, and cocked the hammer, "You need to leave right now!" She whispered with her best mean voice. She put her finger on the trigger. "Don't test me, or..."

"What are you doing?" Ted's voice sounded from behind her, startling her. She jumped with a small scream, and the gun thundered in her hand, shooting a hole through the wall.

Catherine dropped the gun to the floor. There were people screaming all around. She could hear voices in the restaurant yelling, "The Sheriff's down! Someone shot the Sheriff!"

****

Chapter Eight

"Looks like you are going to live."

James leaned back, eyeing the doctor skeptically. "Not if that woman stays around town too much longer."

Doc Merten smiled gently, "Now James, it wasn't her fault."

"People keep saying that... but they aren't the ones getting hurt." He gestured to his eye. "Did you see this? This was half hour before she shot me!"

"I think you're being paranoid."

James frowned and shook his head, "I dunno, Doc. A bullet hole in my leg is telling me I'm right..."

"It's a flesh wound James. It didn't hit a bone, a major blood vessel, or anything else vital for that matter. It will heal fairly quickly."

"Fine. What do I owe you?"

"Nothing, Ted's paying for the house call."

James blew out a breath, "Aw, he doesn't have to do that."

"He feels responsible." Doc started packing his medical bag. "I actually offered to do it free, but he insisted." He pointed at James, "Remember what I told you. Keep it elevated, and try to stay off it as much as you can for a few days. Use a crutch..."

"Do I have to?" James interrupted.

"No, but you're the one who will be in pain, not me." He stepped to the door and stared hard. "And one more thing, stop being paranoid, it's unhealthy. Forgive that little girl, let her say sorry..."

"She already said it a bunch!" James retorted. "She doesn't need to keep repeating herself."

"She will as long as you aren't listening. Just remember what Parson Stone said, 'Forgive those that hurt you.' I think that is apropos in this case."

James eyes narrowed, "What's Indians got to do with this?"

Doc stood, confused for a few moments before his face finally lit up with understanding. "Good one James, I'll have to remember that. Arapahoe, apropos... funny." Chuckling, he left the jail, leaving James wondering what the joke was.

James sighed as he shifted his leg. He had it propped up on his desk, to keep it elevated like the Doc told him to.

He blew out a long breath. He couldn't believe it. The first time he had been shot while on duty as Sheriff, and it was by a woman. And by accident. Everyone in town seemed to think it was pretty funny.

Lucky it was a small town.

He shook his head. He had to admit, it had scared him. He hadn't been shot at for a few years. Even when things were starting to get rough in Lincoln, they weren't shooting at him.

It was downright unnerving.

More than that though, it had brought up some old fears. He'd been fairly young when he went to war, and he had seen hundreds of young men sent home with nothing but crutches and the memory of a leg during the first few years of the war. At that time he could only imagine what their life was going to be like, and he wanted no part of it. He'd had a friend, Billy, who got shot in the leg in the first battle they fought. He'd thought it was just a simple leg wound that needed bandaged, but the doc sawed it off clean anyway. So when he'd been shot during the Battle for Atlanta, he had panicked and pulled a pistol on the doctor, and made him pull the bullet out and bandage him up. He even stayed awake to make sure they left his leg attached. He would have rather died than lose a leg.

Granted, he was older and wiser now. He smiled at that thought; he was all of thirty three... not ancient, but definitely further along than he was at twenty five.

Closing his eyes, he sat back in his chair and sighed, rubbing his face. When he felt the hit, his first thought was that it was Jensen. He'd pulled his gun and had it ready for action. When Ted and Catherine had run in, she had been white as a sheet and kept apologizing over and over. He had yelled, demanding they get out of his line of fire... it took a while before he understood that it was her that had shot him, not robbers in the other room.

She'd started crying by that time, and he'd felt bad as Ted explained it was an accident. He'd tried to joke with her about it, but by that time he was already starting to worry about losing his leg. She didn't take the jokes very well.

He drummed his fingers on the cover of his Bible. He supposed Doc was right. He needed to forgive her. That's what Parson was always saying.

Wait. Where was the Parson? He hadn't noticed him leave earlier. Did he go home? James shook his head as he stared at the crutch Doc had leaned on the wall for him to use. He blew out a long breath and stood, grabbing the crutch.... It'd just be nice if he could have the Parson disarm her before he went over to see her.

****

"Catherine, you need to stop crying."

Catherine lifted her head up from the bed, she knew she looked horrible, but she didn't care. "He thought I did it on purpose."

"No, he doesn't."

"Yes, he does, you heard him." She buried her face back in her pillow. She'd been horrified when the pistol had went off—but when the voice yelled that the Sheriff had been hit... She had rushed over to the restaurant with Ted. First the Sheriff had yelled at her, he'd had his gun in hand; she had thought he was going to shoot her. But then, the look on his face when they told him it was her...

"Ma'am, if you're intent on killing me, I suppose I could stand still to make it easier..."

She broke down in a fresh round of sobs.

"Sweetie, I think he was joking with you. He was trying to make you feel better." Elizabeth sighed loudly, "Anna is here if you want to talk to her."

"I don't want to talk to anyone."

Elizabeth grunted in frustration and left the room, finally leaving her alone. Catherine looked up to make sure the door was closed. She wiped at the tears on her cheek with her sleeve, and sat up on the bed. She couldn't stay here any longer. She needed to just go back home. She would catch the next stage out. She stood quickly and grabbed her bag, sitting it on the bed.

She stared at the bag. There was no use in packing. The next stage wasn't until Monday, four whole days away. Plus, she really didn't want to hurt...

"Catherine?"

Startled, Catherine turned at the voice. Anna had opened the door slightly, and was looking through. "Are you alright dear?"

Catherine broke down in sobs again. "I didn't... want to... talk..." She trailed off as the sobs overtook her sentence.

Anna crossed the room, "There, there." She grabbed her in a hug and held her until her sobs subsided.

Finally in control again Catherine pulled back, "I'm sorry, I..."

"Hush," Anna demanded sternly.

Catherine recoiled in surprise and sat on the bed. She hadn't expected Anna to...

"Now, you listen to me. What you did was an accident. There is no sense in you beating yourself up over it all day."

"But..."

"No buts, I want you to stop." Anna sighed and sat on the bed next to her. "We've been down there listening to you crying, all thinking the same thing. It was an accident, get over it."

Catherine started to speak, but a sharp glance from Anna stopped her.

"Now, you've had a scare, and probably don't need a hundred questions from everyone in town, so you're coming home with me." Anna nodded and stood, "Pack your things—enough for a few days. We'll bring you back Saturday for the Church social."

"Are you sure?" Catherine smiled gratefully. Getting away was what she needed, at least for a few days.

"Yes. Now hurry and pack."

****

"Where are you going?"

James jumped slightly at the voice. The Parson was sitting in a chair on the porch. "Sorry Parson, must've missed you when I came out."

"Didn't answer the question," The Parson grinned wide, an amused expression on his face.

James shrugged, "I was heading over to the store."

"Better not."

"Why not?" James asked, surprised. "I was gonna apologize to that little girl."

"It can wait."

"For what?" Now he was confused. He'd have thought the Parson would be all over an apology, even offering to help him across the street.

"She's upset. Anna's with her." The Parson stood, stretching, "Ted's getting the buckboard ready. Anna wants her to come out to the house for a few days, 'til this blows over."

"Oh."

She'll be back in a few days. Give you time to decide how to apologize." He grinned again, "And make this one without a pistol in your hand."

"That's not fair," James frowned, "I thought it was..."

"I know James, but that young lady didn't."

James sighed and nodded. "Fine. Let me know if there's anything I can do."

****

Chapter Nine

"You have such a beautiful place," Catherine exclaimed as they entered Anna's house. "I didn't expect any houses here to be this... nice." She finished lamely. She thought for a minute, then added, "Not that my sister's house isn't nice..."

"It's alright dear, I understand what you mean." Anna smiled sadly, "My first husband, Clay, was a shipbuilder, and loved to work with wood. He tried to make every project a masterpiece."

"What happened to him?" Catherine asked without thinking, and then blushed. "I'm sorry, I shouldn't have..."

"No, that's fine." She gestured to some chairs in the main room. "Have a seat, and we'll talk."

"What about the Parson?"

"William is putting up the buckboard and helping Thomas with his chores. And Thomas knows better than to come in for a while. Just let me put on some tea."

Catherine nodded, and walked over to the chairs in the main room. The room was quite attractive, with a large bookshelf on one wall. She looked out the large window; there was a wonderful view of the wooded hillside. It was peaceful out here.

She smiled as she considered the trip out to their house. It had been a long trip, but nowhere near as bad as the stage. Thomas had cheered her up by chattering the entire trip about a story in the Bible, one that he claimed was his favorite, It was something about a girl with a hammer pounding a nail into some man's head. She had tried to pay attention, but was too busy laughing at Anna's reaction to his telling of the story.

"Ok, that will take a few minutes to boil."

Startled from her reverie, Catherine turned, "You have such a wonderful view here."

Anna sighed wistfully. "Yes, that was one of the main reasons I talked Clay into settling here. We were heading further west." She nodded at the window, "There are a lot more trees here than town, which changes the scenery." She sat down in one of the chairs. "Fall is beautiful out here when all the trees change color."

"It looks so different from town." Catherine grinned sheepishly, "And there's a lot less dust."

"Yes, it's amazing what a few miles can do for the scenery, but the town is closer to the plains, and we're closer to the mountains." Anna gestured to the chair by hers. "Here, take a seat."

As they both got comfortable, Anna gestured to the room. "We came west just a few years after we were married. Thomas was about a year old. It was during the war; Clay didn't want to get involved, and it had always been his dream to move west." She smiled, sitting back in her chair. "I had no real interest in moving out here. I had grown up in the city, and was used to fancy houses and parties..."

"Where were you from?"

"Boston." She shook her head, "But I was a young girl in love."

Catherine leaned forward, curious, "How old were you?"

"I was just seventeen when Clay and I married. When we came west I was twenty."

Catherine recoiled in surprise, "You're not even thirty yet?"

Anna laughed loudly, "No dear, I'm not..." She grinned, "I guess married life ages you."

Catherine flushed again, embarrassed. "I didn't…"

"Oh, now. I know you weren't trying to be rude." Anna waved a hand dismissively, "Now, where were we… oh yes, we moved here in '63, and Clay built the house. We settled in fairly quick, made friends with the neighbors. Clay even helped a few with their houses." She smiled at the memory, "Clay loved to help people." She shook her head, "Well, one day I was in the barn. We had a cow that was calving… I was out helping, but she was struggling." She sighed, "Clay was out tending to the rest of the herd. We had a storm blowing in, a bad one. I'm not sure how it happened, but while I was busy, the door came open and the wind blew over a lamp. It ignited all the dry straw and hay. The cow got frightened, and jumped. I guess it slammed me into the wall." She paused, breathing deeply before continuing. "Well, I must have been unconscious, because I woke up and the fire was blazing. I was trapped. I started yelling for Clay." She paused again, dabbing at her eye with her handkerchief. "He got in, and got to me. We were coming out when the barn started to collapse. One of the rafters…" She touched her face, "One of the rafters hit me and knocked me down, burning me badly. When I got up, Clay was pinned; unconscious… a large rafter was across his chest." She closed her eyes, "I think he was already dead, but I tried to get him out… I finally had to leave him."

"I'm so sorry. It would be so hard to lose someone you love like that..."

"I lost two." She smiled sadly, "Thomas had a little sister. She was supposed to be born a few months after the fire, but the stress was too much." She blew out a breath. "We had planned to name her Katie. Clay picked out the name. She's buried next to him on the hill."

Catherine shook her head, "That would be so hard."

Anna nodded, "I've made it through. I've heard it said that if you can't see the hand of God, then you can trust the heart of God." She smiled, "Actually, it was William who told me that."

Catherine nodded, and then tilted her head, "Elizabeth said you two just met last year?"

"Well, yes..." She smiled, "...and no. I believe that God brought us together."

Catherine frowned. "How long did you two know each other? How could you be sure of him? I mean..." She blushed, embarrassed, "I was engaged to Alfred for two years, and then at the end I found out that I never really knew him." She shrugged apologetically, "Does that make sense?"

Anna nodded, "Yes." She leaned forward, "Catherine, I've found in my life that some people spend their whole life trying to hide who they really are from everyone. You can never really know someone who has no desire to be known."

Catherine nodded, "But you know William?"

Anna sighed and smiled, "Yes, and more importantly, he knows me." She leaned forward. "See, he didn't just rely on what I appeared to be, he got to know me for who I am." She smiled, "And as a result, I got to know him. That's what drew us together." She gestured to the scarf covering the side of her face, "Some people think that it's only the outside that matters. They will primp and press and work to make that look appealing, but it shorts them. They assume that only the external is important, since that's what they focus on in their own life, that's what they focus on in the lives of others." She sighed, sitting back in her chair. "They end up missing out on relationships with great people, because they were..." She shrugged, "Choosy? Maybe that's the word I want."

Catherine frowned, "Are you saying that I was being choosy with Alfred?" She tilted her head, confused, "Or do you think Alfred was choosy?"

"I've never met Alfred, so understand, this is judgment based only on what you've said, but I've met many people in my life that try to hide what's on the inside, and it's mostly because their inside was so nasty to begin with that they felt obligated to hide it. Kind of like the Pharisee's in the Bible, Jesus called them *'whited sepulchers full of dead men's bones.'* That's most of your 'pretty' people who only focus on the outside."

The kettle in the kitchen started whistling. Anna stood, "Well, time for tea."

As Anna moved into the kitchen, Catherine stayed in her seat and stared out the window, thinking about what Anna had said.

****

Thomas stood on the porch staring at the door. He was hungry, but he could hear his Ma and Miss Catherine talking inside, and he really didn't want to disturb them. He knew Miss Catherine was upset about shooting Mr. James. He had tried to get her mind off it on the ride out, but she still seemed sad.

He nodded to himself. Ma would cheer her up, just like she cheered him up when he was sad. He turned to step off the porch, stopping as he remembered his problem.

He was still hungry.

He sighed and sat on the steps. He could probably sneak in. There was a chance they wouldn't notice him. He could grab a few...

He knew better.

Thomas lay back on the porch, staring at the clouds that dotted the sky. He supposed he could go help Mr. William water the horses; he liked Mr. William, and was glad he had married Ma. He supposed he was like his Pa now, even though he never asked to be called that.

He didn't really remember his real Pa much. He had only been a few years old when he died. He had a few memories, almost like pictures in his head; his Pa looking over his shoulder as he walked down the hill, riding on his horse or kissing him goodnight. He worked hard to keep those pictures locked up in his head so he wouldn't forget them. He was getting some good memories with Mr. William, but didn't want to forget Pa.

He rubbed his eyes and sat up. He was going to get tired if he lay here too long. He wanted to play or do something, but his stomach was so growly, he just needed something to...

He turned his head slightly, listening intently. He could hear the women crying now. He stood and stretched his arms before setting out for the barn. He would have to wait on some food, because with two ladies crying in the house, there was no way he was going anywhere near it.

****

Chapter Ten

"Whooee boy. Looks like you got yerself into some trouble."

James looked up from his desk. Earl was peering in through the open door of the jail. It had been so hot earlier that he had left the door open, hoping for a strong breeze. "What's up, Earl?"

"Not you. Heard a woman shot you." He laughed, "I figgered you forgot to bring flowers or some such nonsense." He crossed the room slowly, favoring his left leg, before setting down heavily in a chair.

"It wasn't like that," James protested.

"Sure, sure." Earl shook his head, "I'm gonna hang my head in shame now. My baby brother can't even protect hisself from a woman..." He leaned in, his eyes narrowing as he stared at James' face. "What happened to your eye?"

James shook his head and sat back. He'd known he would get teased unmercifully from Earl. "Anything else?"

Earl shook his head, "No, I was serious. Did you fall when you got winged?"

"No, who told you I got shot?"

"Parson stopped by, said you might need a brotherly visit. Said you got shot. He didn't say punched."

"It's a long story."

"Looks like you got time. Can't go runnin' off in the midst of it, that's for sure."

James closed his eyes and sighed, "It was an accident."

"Which one? The eye or the leg?"

"Well, both really. The eye was more my fault. I stood in front of a door."

Earl clucked his tongue, "Well, fine. Keep hiding."

James snorted a laugh, "I'm not hiding. I'm right here in the jail where you can find me."

"Yeah, that was easy enough." Earl sighed, settling back in his chair. A few flies buzzed lazily around the room as the two brothers sat in silence.

James picked his Bible up and started reading where he had left off. He had been practicing by moving his mouth as he sounded out the words, but felt awkward with Earl in the room. He was trying to get through the Gospel of John before Sunday, but it wasn't going very fast.

"Still reading the good Book? Parson's been good for you to be around."

James looked up, his eyebrow cocked slightly. "Are you saying I was bad before?"

"No, not bad. Just different."

James put his ribbon back in his Bible to hold his place, and then shut the book slowly. "How different?"

Earl shrugged, "Dunno, just different. Better now, I guess. I just..." He trailed off, "Well, nevermind."

"Oh no." James laughed, sitting forward, "You can't just start talking, and then clam up without an explanation. What do you want to say?"

Earl rubbed his face with his hand before answering. "I like you being here, don't get me wrong. I just wonder if you are wasting your life."

"Wasting my life?" Surprised, James leaned forward. Earl had pressed him to stay here doing this job. What could he possibly complain about now?

Earl grunted, leaning back. "This town ain't growing too fast, and I'm starting to think you're gonna go to waste here."

"I don't get it." James gestured out the door. "You told me this was a good move. That I should stay here..."

Earl raised his hand, cutting him off, "A body can dedicate hisself to something, and in the end it be a waste. I don't wanna see you put everything into this town, then wake up in twenty years and regret it, realizing you shoulda, coulda, woulda done something different. I wasted years chasing gold. Years I coulda..." Earl broke off and shrugged. "You get the idea." He stood suddenly, "Wasn't wanting this to be old home week. I was gonna get supper at Maude's, and thought you'd join me."

James stared for a few moments before nodding, "Alright."

****

James lay in bed, staring at the ceiling as he considered what Earl had said. Was he wasting his life here in Cobbinsville? He hadn't thought so, but he guessed it depended how you looked at it. If you were accomplishing something in life, some goals you had...

He never really set goals in his life though. He had just kind of moved from here to there, based on the opportunities that he was presented with. He was doing what he liked for now, but was it enough? What was he going to do next year? Or in ten years? For that matter, what about when he got old, then what? He knew he always had a place on the ranch, but that was Earl's thing, not his. He hated ranching.

Then there was the question of a family. He knew, subtly, that was what Earl really meant.

He sighed and covered his face with his pillow. He didn't really want to think about a family right now. He had always thought that one day he would get hitched, but it was always a far off thing. He had been happy so far being single.

He knew a lot of men that were single, some were happy and some were flat miserable about it. Out West, womenfolk weren't as plentiful as they were back East. When he was in Lincoln he had known a few men who ordered brides from the East. They had written to a Church, and started 'courtin' a girl by letter. In the end, they paid out a chunk of money to bring the woman West, and married her as soon as she arrived. Some of them seemed happy with the result.

He grimaced, remembering Isaiah Henry's wife. She had been a big girl, with a big appetite. The horses had sighed with relief when she squeezed out of the stage, glad they didn't have to drag her any further. Isaiah had owned a fairly successful restaurant, which was probably the real reason Millicent had agreed to marry poor old Isaiah. He struggled to keep it running after the wedding; his wife ate nine meals a day, and he kept running out of food to serve.

He was fairly sure that Millicent was the reason he had never considered ordering himself a mail order bride.

He rolled to his side, and a sharp pain ran down his leg. Frustrated, he shifted until the pain stopped. Doc had offered him some laudanum, but he had declined. He had seen many people over the years that had become addicted to the stuff, and he had decided to stay away from it as a general rule.

'Course, he'd be better off staying away from Miss Catherine at this point. That would likely improve his health chances more than anything.

He wondered if she ever planned on getting married. Parson had been tweaking him about her, throwing out those subtle hints... at least until she'd shot him. He huffed out a laugh—most everyone had been tweaking him about Catherine since she arrived. Aside from the numerous accidents, she seemed nice enough, but was a tad too...

Pretty?

He yawned, rubbing his eyes and pulling the blanket closer. She was pretty, and maybe that's what scared him. Maybe he thought he deserved a Millicent instead.

Not on ten dollars a month, that was for sure. He couldn't afford to feed a Millicent.

As he drifted off to sleep, he wondered absently how many meals Catherine ate in a day.

****

A cool breeze had blown in sometime during the night, and James woke chilled, with the sun in his face. Annoyed, he pulled the blanket over his head, and rolled over on his side. He wasn't ready to get up and face the world quite yet.

His leg hurt. It had taken some time last night to fall asleep, and it was already throbbing this morning. He stretched it out gingerly, not wanting to open the wound back up.

He lay in bed for several more minutes, listening to the morning sounds of the town. Birds were chirping, and a dog was barking somewhere down the street. He sighed deeply, then pulled the blanket from his face and sat up.

He had a lot to get done anyway.

Today was the big day; the first Church social. He was fairly excited about it, especially since the Parson had been having him help plan the event. He had been getting some games and contests set up, something to get people involved.

He swung his legs from the bed gently, frowning as he noticed that blood had seeped through his bandage overnight. He would need to change it before getting dressed.

****

Chapter Eleven

"**G**o Parson!" James cheered loudly as the Parson and Thomas ran the last lap of the three legged race. They were almost neck and neck with Jed Barlowe and his son.

The games had been going well so far. There had been a great turnout for the social, with people from ranches as far as twenty miles away having shown up.

The Parson and Thomas crossed the finish line a half step in front of Jed, breaking the ribbon to a chorus of wild cheers from the spectators. Doc and his son crossed in third place, immediately tripping and rolling into a pile that caught the next few racers that crossed.

James limped forward, laughing as he skirted the large pile of bodies. He grabbed the Parson by the wrist and lifted his arm up. "Ok people, the winner; Parson William and Thomas!"

Laughing, James clapped briefly, then reached down and offered his hand to the Doc. "Here ya go, old timer."

"Old timer?" Doc chuckled, taking his hand. "I'm not that much older than you."

"No, but you move slow." James pulled, wincing slightly at the pressure in his leg.

"You alright?"

James flashed a quick smile, "Yeah, I'm feeling my age too I guess." He grinned, and patted the Doc on the shoulder. "Good race." He moved off through the small crowd of spectators and limped toward the other side of the field. He needed to get the little kids ready for the sack races.

Hearing another round of cheers, he looked back. The Parson had picked Thomas up and was carrying him on his shoulder like a hero. He grinned and shook his head. Thomas was a good boy. The Parson was lucky to have him.

He felt a pang of emptiness at the thought. He wanted a family, someday at least. A son to play games with, maybe a daughter to read to... He let out a laugh at that thought. Maybe she could read to him instead. At the rate he was learning, he could have a little girl grow up and graduate college before he learned enough.

He shook off the thought. He didn't have time to worry about that now. He turned and started waving his handkerchief, "Race is about to start!" He hollered loudly, signaling the children to come over. He noticed Catherine walking back over toward the Church. He had seen her during the last few events, flushed and excited as she cheered the racers on. She looked like she was having a good time, even though...

He frowned as he remembered the last words he had said to her. He still needed to apologize, but today had been so busy. He sighed, maybe later.

"Mr. James, Mr. James!" Little Ellie Sue Barlowe ran up, laughing loudly as she slammed into him, knocking him to the ground.

He hit the ground hard, trying to catch Ellie Sue before she rolled over his leg, "Whoa girl!" He exclaimed; glad she had come up on his left side.

"I'm ready to race!" She jumped up, laughing and did a little dance in place.

"Oh, Sheriff, I'm so sorry!" Jed ran up, offering a hand.

Pulling himself up, James waved it off, "No damage done." He laughed, and gestured to the sacks on the ground. "But it looks like you just volunteered to help."

****

"Are you enjoying yourself?"

Catherine turned, her sister Elizabeth had walked up so quietly that she hadn't noticed. "Oh Yes! This is great!" Her throat was hoarse from all of the cheering she had been doing, and she was thirsty, but she was having the most fun she could remember having in ages.

Elizabeth patted her shoulder, "I'm glad to hear it."

Catherine flashed her sister a dazzling smile, "I'm getting thirsty though. I've done way too much cheering today."

"I think they put out some tea by the Church."

Catherine gave her sister a quick hug, then started walking toward the Church. She had never thought a Church social could be this fun, especially in Cobbinsville. Almost everything about this place had surprised her since she arrived; the town, the people...

She looked behind her, spotting James on the other side of the field. He was waving his handkerchief, yelling to the children about the sack race. She smiled, and turned back toward the Church.

She had been surprised to see him hobbling around the field today. He seemed to be in good spirits, and was the judge of most of the games. She guessed he was healing pretty quickly to be on his feet already. She still felt bad, but she hadn't gotten the courage to talk to him yet. She was waiting for the right time.

She sighed, shaking her head. She knew that it really wasn't about the 'right time', but more about being too chicken to face him, afraid he was still upset.

It was understandable. After all, she had shot him, even if it was an accident, it was bad. Anna had told her to not worry so much, that he had already forgiven her, but she wasn't too sure about that. When Alfred got upset he would stay mad for a long time. When she had told Anna about that, Anna's answer had been simple. *'James isn't Alfred.'*

Anna had been such a blessing the last few days. They had talked late the first night, and then spent all day yesterday talking while baking treats for the social.

Of course, Anna had also spent a fair amount of time keeping Thomas out of the baked goods. She smiled, remembering last evening; it had been a long day of baking, and she and Anna had been sitting at the table talking about what music they were going to play today at the social. Movement had caught her eye. Thomas was on the floor, crawling silently from the kitchen with a cookie hanging from his mouth. He had looked up at her wide eyed, pleading for her silence with a glance. She had burst out in laughter, and covered her face, but Anna had thought she had broken down crying about the music. By the time she could tell the story with a straight face Thomas had already made three more trips!

Stopping at the refreshment table, Catherine poured herself a glass of tea, and then turned to watch the games. The children were climbing into some potato sacks, preparing for a sack race. James was helping a little girl get into hers, since she kept losing her balance and falling out.

She smiled, absently wondering what kind of father he would be, and then choked on her tea, wondering where that thought had come from.

****

James took another bite of cobbler as he watched the small crowd of people. He was sitting off to the side, on a bench with his leg propped up. It was aching pretty good after all of the walking around he had done earlier. He had been sitting at the main table for a while, but the constant questions about his leg, followed closely by questions about his eye... well, he just preferred to be by himself right now.

"Whatcha doin', Mr. James?"

James looked over, startled by the interruption. Thomas had appeared next to him. He was holding a plate of food in his hands. "You like to sneak up on people, don't ya?"

Thomas grinned wide, "Yes sir. I'm real quiet."

James chuckled, and patted the bench next to him, "Sit a spell. Looks like you got some good food."

Thomas sighed dejectedly as he sat, "Ma won't let me have cobbler until I finish my chicken." He started picking at the food on his plate, obviously not interested in even tasting his chicken.

"Oh, that's too bad." James looked back out at the crowd. It was a happy group tonight. A lot of dancing and eating. They had moved the Church piano outside and Catherine was playing a lively tune while a group was square dancing.

"Why are you sitting by yourself?" Thomas asked suddenly.

James shrugged, "Just watching the fun. Why?" He took a bite of his cobbler.

"Ma said you need to get a wife."

James started coughing as he choked on his cobbler, "What?"

Thomas stared at him, concerned. "Are you ok?"

He held up his hand, "Fine..." He croaked out, and then cleared his throat. "Your Ma said what?"

Thomas shrugged, and continued picking at his chicken. "She said you need a wife. I heard her and Mr. William talking earlier. She said Miss Catherine was a nice girl, so maybe you should start there." He looked up at him, wide eyed and innocent.

James blinked a few times. He couldn't believe that Anna would... well, then again, he could. "I'm sure Miss Catherine is a nice girl. You know, we've met a few times..."

"She's the one that shot you in the leg, right?"

"Well, yes. But that was an accident."

"And she gave you that black eye?"

James' hand involuntarily lifted to his face, "Yes, but that was an accident too."

Thomas was silent for a moment, then added, "Didn't she hit you with a trunk, too?"

James' head started to throb, "Yes, she did..."

Thomas sighed, "Ma told me when little Sarah Mae kept hitting me it was 'cause she liked me." He shook his head sadly as he stood, "I guess Miss Catherine really likes you. I'm gonna see if Ma'll let me have some cobbler yet." With that, he walked off toward the food tables.

James sat on the bench for a few moments, watching Thomas move back across the yard, wondering why exactly he had just had that conversation.

****

"Was that really all you wanted me to do was talk to Mr. James?"

"Yes it was." Anna placed a large piece of cobbler on Thomas' plate. "And you did very well, Thomas. You are such a good boy."

"What's going on?"

Anna turned sharply, trying to look innocent, "Oh, William. Nothing is going on. I was just giving Thomas some cobbler."

William eyed the plate, "That's a pretty large piece of cobbler, isn't it?"

Anna gave him a coy half smile, "No... Thomas earned this piece." She straightened her dress, "I'm going to talk to a few people."

William shrugged, "That's fine, dear."

Anna moved off, wanting to talk to Catherine as soon as she was done playing the piano.

****

"Howdy."

Catherine looked up from her plate. The Sheriff had walked over, and was standing nearby with his hat in hand. "Hello Sheriff Matthews."

He frowned as she answered. She guessed he was still upset with her. She held up her hands, "I'm so sorry about the other day."

He shook his head, "I wasn't... I didn't mean..." He broke off, flustered. "I just wanted to say sorry is all."

She started, surprised, "For what? I'm the one that owes you..."

"No," He cut her off with a curt gesture, "I didn't act right to you the other day. It was an accident, and you were trying to apologize, and I didn't..." He shook his head again, "I didn't accept it right. I made you upset, and that was wrong."

"You don't owe me an apology, Sheriff."

His frown deepened, "No, I do. My Pa raised me to be respectful to womenfolk, especially their feelings, and I wasn't." He shook his head, "See, the other day you and me were friends, now it's all formal, 'Sheriff Matthews' and all. I'm formal to people I don't know, and people I don't like, and I didn't think you were either."

"Oh." She smiled softly, "Well, I accept your apology, if it helps." She paused for a moment, and added, "James."

"Thank you, Catherine." He stood there for a moment, looking uncomfortable, and then gestured to the piano. "You play real nice."

"Thank you, but I'm really not that good." Catherine frowned, remembering his leg, and gestured to a nearby chair. "Please sit down; your leg must be hurting."

Shrugging, he sat down on a bench. "It's not that bad, I was just up on it too much today."

"You were quite busy with the games."

"Yes Ma'am, I was. I didn't realize that being a judge was that hard of work."

They shared a quiet laugh, and then sat in silence for a few moments, watching the people. Some of them; the ones that lived further away, were packing up to go home.

He cleared his throat, "So... did you try any cobbler?"

She smiled at his attempt at conversation. "Um, no. I was eating some of Anna's chicken, but it got cold while I played."

"Sorry. It was good though." He fell silent again for a moment, and then added, "You want me to get you something to eat?"

****

Anna stood by the corner of the Church watching the couple talk quietly. She heard footsteps coming up behind her.

"Now, what are you smiling about?"

She answered without turning, "Now William, what makes you think I'm smiling?"

"Because I know you." He wrapped his arms around her, pulling her close. "Matchmaker." He teased softly.

She leaned backwards into his embrace. "I just want them to be happy."

"Is that what makes you happy?"

She laughed softly, "No, William. You make me happy."

"Well, I'm glad for that." William chuckled softly, "I think next social we'll have all the single ladies make a sack lunch and raffle it off to the highest bidder."

"We'll have to get a few more single ladies in town for that."

"We have Maude. She's single, with a thriving restaurant."

"She's an easy sixty years old. I don't think she's looking for a husband."

William laughed aloud, "Then you haven't seen her when Earl comes to town for a bite to eat."

She turned, surprised. "Are they sweet on each other?"

"Great, now I've done it." William shook his head in mock sadness. "Poor people will never know what hit them."

"Oh, you!" She playfully punched him in the arm, and then turned to watch James and Catherine, but her mind was already racing ahead. She was going to have a long talk with Earl in the morning.

****

Chapter Twelve

James had just finished his dinner when he heard the stage begin its descent into town. He wiped his face with his napkin and yelled, "Thanks Maude," as he stood and stretched. It had been a long day already, and he was ready for bed. He smiled as he pulled his watch from his pocket; bedtime wouldn't be for another seven or so hours. He shook his head and walked out of the restaurant.

The stage was just pulling up to the front of the store. "Hey Sheriff." Jim hollered as the stage stopped in a cloud of dust. He was an old buffalo hunter who often rode shotgun for Ray.

James nodded, "Hey Jim. Ray."

Ray had swung down from his seat, and opened the stage door. "Alright people, we got 15 minutes.

Food is in the restaurant, and the outhouse is in the back."

James stopped suddenly as a pretty young woman stepped from the stage. A young man was standing, offering his hand to help her step down, but she ignored the hand and stepped down on her own. She looked around, taking in the town with a clinical gaze before moving toward the store.

Dejected, the young man stood forlorn, watching her as she walked briskly up the steps and entered the store.

Ray called out, "Hey lady, don't forget your bags!"

James turned back. Ray had climbed on top of the stage, and was staring at the store, shaking his head. He looked over, "Sheriff, lemme holler at you for a minute."

James moved over to the stage. "What's up, Ray? One of your riders leave their bags?"

"Nah, she'll be out I guess. You see that young feller get his ears pinned back? He's been talking her up for forty miles, but she won't have none of it." He chuckled and shook his head. "No, I just thought I'd pass on the latest news. Jensen robbed a bank over in Sherman. Him and his gang blasted their way out of town."

James frowned, "Sherman? That's a good distance away... probably a hundred odd miles."

"Yeah, it's a pretty good ways down the line. Seems like you won't have to worry after all."

"Thanks, Ray." James gestured toward the store, "I'll make sure the lady claims her bags."

The young man was staring wistfully at the door, as if unsure whether he should follow. Chuckling, he limped toward the store, passing the young man. Ted would be thrilled to hear the news about Jensen. He'd been on edge all week.

****

"Stage coming in!" Ted hollered from the back room. Catherine grunted a reply without looking up from her book. She had heard it pull in already. As a matter of fact, she had been listening to the stage since it first started coming down the hill. She hated when the stage came in. Rude passengers, the ones that chose not to eat at the restaurant, usually came in complaining about their trip. On top of that, it stirred up the already pervasive dust, and made it that much more difficult to breathe.

She missed the cobblestone streets of Philadelphia, the lush houses, the parties...

Sighing, she started reading her book again. Not that it was much of a book; it was a dime novel, left in the restaurant by a passenger last week. '*Indian Jim and the tale of the Minnesota Massacre.*' It was about a Sioux uprising in Minnesota and a raid on a

German village in 1862. She had no idea how much of it was embellished, but it passed the time.

She had never been much of a reader back home. She knew how to read of course, but had just never devoted that much time to it. She had always been too busy; parties, tea and... Alfred.

She frowned thoughtfully, realizing it had been some time since she had given him serious thought. When she first came west every little thing reminded her of him, and not a moment had gone by without a pang in her heart, but now it seemed like it was just the occasional bad memory.

She supposed it was like Anna had told her, that one day at her house. 'Catherine, people that are worth remembering will always be a fond memory in the background, but people that aren't will fade like a bad dream, with just the memory that they weren't worth it.'

The bell on the door rang as it opened, bringing her back to the present. Sighing again, she refused to look up, not wanting to deal with another complaint.

"Excuse me, miss?"

Catherine, unable to pretend she hadn't heard, looked up. There was a young woman standing by the door; a pretty young woman, fairly close to her own age. She was brushing the dust from her dress. Catherine smiled; the woman had good taste in clothing. She owned one that was similar. "May I help you?"

"I'm sorry to bother you, but I'm looking for Daniel Merten."

Catherine frowned, thinking hard. The name sounded familiar, but she... "Wait, you mean Doc?"

The young woman laughed, "Yes, that's him."

"I'm sorry; I haven't seen him in town for a few days." At the young woman's puzzled look, she offered, "His place is a few hours ride from town."

"Oh." It was the young woman's turn to be puzzled. "He told me he lived in Cobbinsville, I assumed it meant in Cobbinsville." She shook her head, "No matter, we'll figure it out." She crossed the room and offered her hand, "I'm sorry I was rude, my name is Margaret Merten, Doctor Margaret Merten. I'm his daughter."

Catherine took her hand, surprised. "I'm so sorry, I heard him talking about his daughter to Ted... I assumed you would be a child." She looked around apologetically, "I'm sorry he's not here..."

"Oh, that's my fault," Margaret exclaimed, smiling. "I wanted to surprise him. He thinks I'm coming next month."

The door chimed again, and both girls turned to face the door. James limped in, still favoring his leg, and immediately whipped his hat from his head. "Ma'am... Ma'am." He focused on Catherine, "Is Ted here?"

"In the back." She came from behind the counter, "James, this is Doc's daughter, Doctor Margaret

Merten. Doctor, this is James Matthews, the Sheriff of Cobbinsville."

Margaret laughed, "Sheriff, it is good to meet you."

James nodded slightly, "Ma'am."

"Do you think you could ride out and tell the Doc that she's here?" Catherine asked.

James nodded, "It'd be my pleasure. I just need to holler at Ted first." He nodded again, "Ladies," and limped toward the back room.

Catherine turned to Margaret and smiled, "See, all taken care of Doctor..."

"Oh, now!" Margaret interrupted suddenly, "My friends call me Maggie, and I think we are going to be just that." She watched James disappear into the back room. "He's nice looking." She frowned, "Did he injure himself?"

Catherine blushed, "He...um... Was shot a few days ago."

"Oh my!" Maggie turned to face her, "Was it a bandit?"

"No... not exactly."

"Then what happened?"

Catherine, thoroughly embarrassed, looked down at the floor. "I was... um, holding a gun, and it... fired."

"You shot him?"

"Yes." She answered softly. She could feel her face burning.

Maggie laughed loudly. Catherine looked up; Maggie was doubled over in laughter, holding her side. "That is so bad. I'm glad he wasn't seriously injured, but that is just too funny."

"Well, it was kind of frightening when it happened," Catherine protested softly. She felt a small smile tugging at the corner of her mouth. Maggie's laughter was almost infectious.

"Of course it was." Maggie grabbed her shoulder, "That is great. I needed a good laugh after that trip." She wiped at a tear trailing from her eye. "Now, I know we are going to be friends."

****

Laramie, WY

"We ride south."

Carter looked up from the paper he was reading, "Mexico?"

Jensen nodded slowly, "Yeah, I think we've led them in this direction long enough. We'll cut south, and then run south and west."

Carter nodded; he was tired of running, period. He wanted to be somewhere he could relax, and not look over his shoulder. "We heading straight there?"

Jensen shook his head, "Didn't get enough money. We'll need to stop by a place or two on the way."

"They'll just turn right around and foller us!" Vic exclaimed from his seat.

"Shesh up you fool. I got a plan." He grinned, "We're gonna pick a few places way off the line. Take 'em days to figure it out."

Vic looked over at Carter, "You think that's wise?"

Jensen leaped forward, slapping Vic across the cheek. The sharp snap of the impact cause heads to turn in the bar. "Don't you ever question me again!" He muttered threateningly.

Carter caught Vic's eye and nodded imperceptibly. They'd do it Jensen's way... for now.

****

Chapter Thirteen

" **. . . a**re talking about a man who stepped out of a boat in the middle of a storm to walk on the water... he was obviously not a coward."

Catherine looked down, staring at the small spot on her dress. She was usually interested in the Parson's sermons, but today she was really struggling to concentrate on the message.

She glanced sideways; Anna was intently watching her husband as he talked about Peter, seemingly oblivious to Catherine's struggles at focusing.

She sighed softly and looked down at her Bible. It wasn't that the sermon wasn't interesting; she just had so much running through her mind that it made it hard to sit still and listen. Of course, she knew she wasn't the only one who was struggling. Over the past several weeks she had gotten to know most of the other members of the Church, and could tell what many of them would be doing without looking up. Mrs. Lindsey, the large woman with the aisle seat, would be haughtily rolling her eyes as the Parson preached, thus signifying that the person the Parson was discussing was much less spiritual than herself. Thomas would be playing with something, but trying to look like he was paying attention. Widow Johnson would be asleep in her pew, her neck bent at an impossible angle... she continued through the congregation before looking up. She smiled as she checked each individual, pausing when she reached the Doc's pew. Maggie was sitting ramrod straight next to Caroline as the Parson spoke, listening attentively.

Catherine grimaced, wondering if she should feel bad for not paying as thorough attention to the service as Maggie was instead of letting her mind wander.

Her eyes cut back to James. He had just taken something away from Thomas, and was directing him to listen. She smiled softly. She couldn't believe the transformation he had undergone in her mind over the last several weeks; from the day she first met him, stinky and dirty from a long ride, to now. She could see something deeper, something...

He noticed her watching and smiled, then held up a feather; obviously what he had just taken from Thomas. Blushing, she looked back at the Parson, and tried to listen. He was talking about the danger of putting your will in front of God's will for your life. She had evidently missed the last point, but she tried to focus on what he was saying to catch up.

The Parson was pointing out into the crowd, "...was why Peter denied God. It wasn't fear, or even ignorance, it was simply that he wanted things his way, and that didn't match with God's way. What about you? Are you wanting to do things God's way? Or are you still stuck in a 'this is what I want out of life' mindset?"

Catherine sat up, suddenly interested, wishing she had paid attention to the last point. She had read the story of Peter often, and had even heard it preached several times, but it was always that he was afraid of being arrested. She had never thought of it like this, that he was just too busy doing things his way.

What about her? She frowned as she considered the Parson's question. Was she unwilling to follow the Lord's will because she was too busy wanting to follow her own will?

She thought back to the last few years of her life. When had she ever bothered to see what God wanted from her life? After all, she was a Christian, wasn't she? Didn't she owe Him something?

Pieces from sermons she had heard the last few weeks suddenly started to convict her with their message; things she had forgotten suddenly brought back to her mind as she suddenly faced her own... was it disobedience? Or just self-will?

Wasn't self-will, at its core, disobedience?

She looked down at her Bible, suddenly ashamed as she realized where her own self-will had gotten her. Many nights of blaming God for her embarrassment with Alfred, when she had never stopped to question whether he was the one that God would have her with. How much of her life had she wasted on a relationship that she wanted, but it was so evident that God didn't? Sure, she had already started to forget about him, but she was still faced with the reason she had ended up with him in the first place. Her own willfulness.

As she looked down at the Bible on her lap, her eyes were drawn to a verse. *"If we confess our sins, he is faithful and just to forgive us our sins, and to cleanse us from all unrighteousness."* As she read it, she knew what she should do. She closed her eyes and prayed, and asked the Lord to forgive her self-will.

As she prayed, she felt the hot sting of tears as they ran down her cheek. There was a part of her that worried what others might think if they saw her, but she refused to give in to that side of herself. That was pride talking. Look where that had gotten her. Two years of her life wasted.

She felt a hand on her shoulder, and knew that Anna was next to her, praying for her. Anna had probably known since the first time they talked. She had been so easy with her counsel as she tried to tell her, tried to show her, but she hadn't listened.

Catherine finished praying and felt... well, almost cleaner as a result. She swallowed hard, making the commitment to not fall into that trap again.

She looked up and noticed that the Parson was finishing his sermon. She glanced over at Anna and smiled. She would have to talk with her after the service, because she wanted some counsel on what to do next. The last thing she wanted was to repeat the same mistakes she had already made.

****

James sat quietly in his pew and stared thoughtfully at the pulpit. The Parson had dismissed Church several minutes before, and most of the people had left. Many were outside still fellowshipping. While the people who lived closer went home to eat, many of the families who lived further away had brought a picnic lunch, and stayed to eat it on the grounds before taking the long trip home.

But he was still thinking about the message.

He had heard many sermons over the years. Sermons that challenged him to do more; be a better Christian, soldier, son, friend, all of those things, but this time he had been faced with the question of his own obedience, and felt like he was found wanting at this point.

That was part of the reason he liked the Parson to begin with, he didn't mince words. He told you what you needed to hear, and left you to decide what you were going to do with it.

Now he just needed to decide what he was going to do with it.

He wanted to talk some with the Parson, but he was already deep in conversation with Mrs. Lindsey, and it didn't look like it was going to end soon.

Sighing, he looked around the small Church, a smile tugging at the corner of his mouth as he remembered the amount of labor it had taken to build it earlier that year. They had hauled lumber down from the sawmill at Fort Steele, and many of the men in the surrounding area had come out to help raise it up. It was initially supposed to be smaller, but as they planned and prepared people kept coming up with improvements, better ideas, and more importantly, donations of time, tools and money to assist in the process. They had even raised the money for windows that opened, and a fancy colored window at the back behind the pulpit.

As he focused on the front, he suddenly noticed the whisper of conversation coming from the side area. He stood, blushing as he noticed Anna and Catherine were praying by the piano.

He slipped quietly toward the back of the Church, and exited the building. He didn't want them to think he was eavesdropping or anything, so he figured he'd just talk to the Parson later.

As he walked toward the jail, he felt a small smile tug at the corner of his mouth, fairly certain that he was not the only one in the Church that the message had spoken to.

****

Catherine walked slowly back to her sister's house feeling, for the first time in a long time, free of the weight she had been carrying. She and Anna had spoken at length about decisions and how to find God's will for her life. Anna had given her some solid, practical tips, including one strong admonition about relationships.

Anna had looked sharply at her when she asked about men. *"Now, we've already discussed that Alfred fellow before, but consider him an example."*

"An example?"

"Sure," Anna had flashed her half smile, *"Nobody is useless, they can always be used as a bad example. Now, let me ask you this; what was Alfred's life like? Was he working for himself, or for others?*

"What do you mean?" She had asked.

"Well," Anna gestured to the Church, "Did he often focus on the things that made him look good, especially by pointing out flaws in others?" She shook her head, "You never want a man like that." She stood, stretching out her leg. "Catherine, personally I think you should be looking for a relationship. I don't think that God expects you to be alone."

Catherine scoffed, "I'm just not sure I should be looking, given my track record."

"Honey, just because you made a mistake with one, that doesn't mean you should stop. Just make sure you pick the right kind of man this time."

"But what do you mean, the 'right kind' of man?"

Anna had smiled, "Easy, the right kind will be one that you see putting others before himself. That is the kind of man that is right."

As Catherine neared her sister's house, her eyes were drawn to the squat, ugly building across from the store. She wasn't blind. It was fairly obvious that Anna was hinting about James. The question was whether he was really the man God was directing her to.

****

Chapter Fourteen

Catherine hummed softly as she dusted the shelves. She wondered how Elizabeth had gotten anything done before she came to town, considering how much time she was spending with the feather duster. It had become pretty well automatic for her now, to pick up the duster and start swatting the shelves at regular intervals. At least if she were destined to be a small town, store dusting spinster, she would be good at it.

She grimaced, shaking her head, not sure where that thought came from. Initially she had only come West for a visit, albeit an extended one, and had really intended on going home at some point. There was still a part of her that couldn't wait to return home, especially when she was dusting.

She paused and glanced over at the clock; it was almost noon, almost time for James to come over to the restaurant for dinner.

She couldn't help but smile when she thought about James. He had stopped into the store several times so far this week. He had mentioned that Doc ordered him to spend some time off of his horse, since he had overdone it at the Church social.

She felt bad when she thought about the social. It was only a few days after 'the accident,' and he had been on his feet most of the day, against Doc's orders, trying to make the games special for the kids. He had never let on to anyone that he was hurting. She didn't even realize it that night when she talked to him, but had overheard Doc bragging to Ted about it the other day, about how selfless James was.

She finished dusting and tossed the feather duster under the counter before sitting down on her stool. Sighing, she stared out the front window of the store. She had never considered selflessness as a positive trait before, but it made sense.

When she had talked to Anna about Alfred, Anna had told her that the type of man she should be looking for was one that put the needs of others ahead of his own, and not one that put his own needs first. That definitely was not Alfred. Alfred made no qualms about putting himself up on a pedestal.

Of course, it was more than just self-emulation. She had thought James would never have forgiven her for shooting him. She knew Alfred wouldn't have, but she remembered what Anna had told her.

'James isn't Alfred.'

All the more proof of how selfless he was.

She smiled softly to herself. Maybe she was rushing with the spinster idea. Although he hadn't said anything suggesting anything more than friendship, James did seem to be much more attentive to her...

So, maybe something could develop.

Shaking her head, she picked up her book. It was a poetry collection by Keats that Anna had leant her. She was re-reading one named 'Isabella.' It was the sad tale of a woman who lost her true love to her murderous brothers. She had missed him so much that she went searching for him. When she had finally found the body and brought back his head, she kept it in a pot, so he would always be near. She even planted basil in the pot to help hide it from her brothers.

She had cried the first time she read it, it was so touching. She opened the book, and had just started to read when she heard the sound of a buckboard coming down the hill. She was getting good at picking out the different sounds, but not as good as Elizabeth.

She looked back down at her book, it would take several minutes for whoever it was to arrive, so she

Sparks of Affection

was determined to finish a few more stanzas while she waited.

****

James looked up as the door opened. He smiled as Doc Merten entered the jail, followed by his daughter. He stood quickly, wincing at the pain in his leg. "Hello Doc, Miss...Doctor Merten."

Maggie laughed lightly, "Well, I usually go by 'Doc' myself, but that would get a tad confusing, wouldn't it? Just call me Maggie, Sheriff."

"Yes Ma'am, Maggie. You can call me James." He looked at the Doc, who had just sat his bag on the desk. "What's going on today, Doc?"

"Just coming around to check on your leg, especially after all the strain you put on it last week. I wanted to make sure it was healing right." He opened his bag, and pulled out his head reflector, and positioned it on his head. "I thought I'd bring Maggie around to watch me work."

"Oh, Ok." James smiled, and sat back in his chair. He was glad he had been hit in the calf, and not any higher. He remembered Jack Donovan, a man he had met in the hospital after the Battle for Atlanta. Jack had got shot in the backside, and anytime a woman nurse came to check his bandage, he would curl up in a corner of the tent and refuse to let her look. He grinned at the memory, and scooted his chair back, then gently pulled off his boot.

134

Doc pulled up a short stool, and sat it in front of James. "Bullet wound to distal *Gastrocnemius*..." He paused, thinking, "...eight days ago. Minor tearing of outer head, no damage to tibia or fibula." Doc continued talking as James pulled up the leg of his pants. "It's healing well overall, but it looks like the wound is still draining through the wrapping." He looked up, "Tsk Tsk, James, I've told you to stay off of this."

"I did... this week."

"Right." Doc unwrapped the wound, and continued describing the treatment that he had performed so far.

James sat straight, looking ahead as the Doc prodded the wound. Maggie had leaned in close as they discussed the stitching. He felt awkward as they discussed his leg, ignoring him like he wasn't even in the room.

"Can you stand?"

"What?" Startled, James looked down. Maggie was staring at him, "I wanted to see the exit wound, can you stand?"

"Um, sure." He stood, now feeling like a calf at auction, and turned to give them a better view. They continued talking, oblivious to his discomfort, as he stood facing the back wall.

"Alright James, I'm going to wrap the wound again. You can sit."

James sat as the Doc bandaged his leg once more. He glanced sideways at Maggie, who was watching with detached interest. "So, Maggie. Did you deal with a lot of bullet wounds back East?"

She shrugged, "A few, and a few other type of injuries, but mostly I dealt with obstetrics." At his blank look, she added, "Women giving birth." She grinned, "I came West to see more interesting patients."

"Oh." He nodded, wide eyed, unsure of how to respond. Honestly, she kind of scared him a little.

"Well, James, I think you'll continue to live." The Doc had finished wrapping his leg, and stood. "Let me know if anything changes." He pulled off the reflector, and shoved it in his bag. "Oh, and by the way, what are you doing tomorrow?"

James shrugged, "Well, tomorrow's Saturday... I'll check in on a few of the closer ranches and drop in on Widow Johnson. Probably have supper at Maude's."

"Well, you ought to ride out and have supper with us. Caroline just said the other day it had been a while since we had company."

James nodded, "Sure thing. I'll be out that way late afternoon."

Doc nodded, and then gestured to the door. "Alright, Maggie. Let's get out of the good Sheriff's hair for now." He grinned, and opened the door, allowing Maggie to step out first. He turned and winked, "See you tomorrow, young man."

Offering a small wave, James stood for a few minutes, wondering what in the world Doc was up to.

****

Catherine looked up as the Doc and Maggie entered the store. She smiled and set her book on the counter. "Doc, Maggie, I thought I saw your buggy pull in earlier. It's nice to see you."

Doc smiled, "Nice to see you as well, Catherine. Is Ted here?"

"He's next door. Maude was having some trouble with her pump."

"Ah. I think I'll poke my head in over there." He turned to Maggie, "You want to stay here and socialize?"

Maggie grinned, "Sure."

Elizabeth stepped out from the storage room. "Oh, piffle. You girls go next door and grab some tea. I'll mind the store."

Catherine smiled, "Are you sure?"

"Of course. Now shoo."

Catherine looked over to Maggie, "Want to get tea?"

Maggie shrugged, "Coffee sounds better."

They followed Doc over to Maude's. As they entered, Maude met them at the door. "Ah, ladies. Will you have some tea?"

Catherine smiled, "Yes, please. And a coffee."

"Fine, fine dearies. Pick a spot and I'll bring it out to you."

They picked a table, and sat down. Maude brought out their drinks, and some cookies. They sat in silence for a few minutes while they listened to Ted and the Doc talking in the back.

"So, how do you like it here?" Maggie asked innocently as she tapped the table with her finger.

Catherine sipped her tea, wincing as the hot liquid burned her lip. "Honestly?"

"Not that well?"

"I didn't say that," Catherine protested, looking around. She didn't want Maude to hear their conversation.

"Maude stepped into the back already." Maggie offered, as if reading her mind.

"Oh." Catherine turned back to Maggie. "The people here are really nice."

"What people there are, right?"

Catherine nodded, blowing on her tea to cool it. She had to admit, Maggie got it right with that statement. "I'm just used to being around more people."

Maggie grinned, "A lot more people."

They shared a quiet laugh. Catherine shook her head. "Finally, someone that understands what it's like. Elizabeth is always talking about how great the quiet is, and I keep telling her that it's just not what I'm used to."

"I'm having the same problem with my father. He likes being a country doctor, but I don't think that's for me." She made a face, "Oh look, Ed fell on his pitchfork, and Mary has a wart." She sat back in her chair. "I figured there would be something more, at least some gunshot wounds to tend." Leaning in, she playfully slapped Catherine's hand. "Other than the one inflicted by a certain young lady from the store, that is."

Catherine blushed, "It was an accident."

"I know, I was just teasing." Maggie sighed. "I think the Sheriff is coming out to the house for supper Saturday, as a matter of fact."

"Really?" Catherine kept her face neutral as she blew on her tea again.

"Does that bother you?"

"Does what bother me?"

Maggie rolled her eyes, "Come on Catherine, I saw how you two look at each other."

Catherine felt herself color slightly, "I'm not sure what you mean. We're just friends. It's not like we're courting or anything. "

"Uh-huh." Maggie grinned. "Well, he's a handsome one, that's for certain. It's a wonder he's still single." She took a sip of her coffee. "My father keeps bringing him up in conversation, mentioning him over and over; *'Oh, did you know the Sheriff did this'* or *'Isn't he a nice man'* or the worst was *'He's what women would call handsome, right?'*" She shook her head, laughing. "I'm not sure half the time if he thinks I should court him, or if he wants to court the Sheriff himself."

Catherine gasped with laughter. She could imagine what it was like, considering she got the same treatment all the time from Elizabeth. And Ted, and Anna, and even Maude. She took another sip of her tea. "The question is, what do *you* think of him?"

Maggie sighed, "Not my type." She took a sip of coffee, and set her cup on the table. "Don't get me wrong, he seems like a great guy, just not for me."

"Really?" Catherine frowned, curious. "Why is that?"

"It's a couple of things, really. I guess the first part really applies to most men out here. They seem to have this, 'a woman can't really do a man's job' thing going in their mind. I fought hard against that to get where I am, and couldn't really see myself in a relationship with a man who carries it."

"James acts like that?" Catherine asked, surprised. She didn't think he was like that... of course, she wasn't doing what most people thought of as a man's job, either.

"Well, not that I've seen." Maggie paused a moment before adding, "Yet."

"Hmmm." Catherine raised an eyebrow, "You said a couple of things?"

"Well, the other is simple. I'm just not sure I can do the 'live in a boring small town' thing for very long. James seems quite content with that, but I wouldn't be." She grinned again, "How about you? Would you consign yourself to a lifetime of small-town...?" She trailed off with an exaggerated shrug, "Drudgery, or whatever it is? Do you think he's worth it?"

Catherine gave a small shrug, and Maggie continued talking, oblivious to her response. She talked about men she had met back East, places she had been, and things she had done, quite acceptably filling in the quiet until Doc was done in the kitchen.

They said their goodbyes, with promises to get together again soon.

As Catherine walked back over to the store, her eyes were drawn to the squat, ugly building across the street with several questions burning in her mind... Was God directing her to James, or was she just trying to replace Alfred on her own? And if James was who God wanted her with, did He really expect her to stay permanently in Cobbinsville?

****

Chapter Fifteen

James tugged on the reins as he rode down the hill. It had been a pleasant morning, a lot cooler than it had been the last few months. Off in the distance he could see a line of trees; he knew that they would be shifting color before long. He couldn't wait for that.

Of course, right behind that would be winter; more trudging through the snow as he did his rounds, more chance of frostbite and freezing to death and...

He shook off the depressive line of thought. He was feeling edgy today, and didn't quite know why. He'd made his rounds to the local ranches; his visit with Widow Johnson had been uncharacteristically short today, as he was interested in getting an early start heading for Doc's.

Well, that and the fact that he had no interest in giving her another opportunity to pry into his personal life. He guessed that was part of the problem. It seemed like everywhere he turned, someone was more interested in his personal life than he was.

He shook his head, and focused on the ride. It was a good ways out to the Doc's. He hadn't been really specific about the time for him to show, so he was taking it slow, checking out the scenery. It gave him plenty of time to think. Unfortunately, all he could think about was Catherine.

She had been somewhat distant the last few days. Well, he corrected himself, yesterday and today anyway. He had thought she was over the whole shooting thing, but now it seemed like she had something else stuck in her craw. He'd seen her when he was leaving Maude's the day before, and she never said a word to him. This morning he stopped in the store to get a bit of sugar to take to Mrs. Johnson and she would barely look in his direction.

As a matter of fact, she acted like he had offended her in some way. He tried to think back to their previous conversations. He had to admit that they were pretty boring; he'd talk about the weather or people and whatnot, but that was all he knew.

Maybe she was mad 'cause he was boring?

He sighed, shaking his head. He was never going to understand womenfolk.

****

James took a sip of his coffee, struggling to come up with a way to start a conversation. Up until now he would have said that Catherine was easy to talk with, but Maggie...

Well, Maggie still scared him a bit.

After supper, Caroline had cleared the dishes, and insisted on doing them herself. Then Doc abandoned him at the table with Maggie, retiring to the living room to read while He and Maggie stared uncomfortably at each other.

She didn't even play checkers, which was normally his first line of retreat when he couldn't think of something to say.

He shook his head. He guessed both women were going to be mad at him. He supposed he was going to have to work on his socializing skills.

"So..." He finally offered, "What is medical school like for woman?"

Maggie stared at him for a moment before answering, her mouth tight. "Well, probably about the same as it is for a man."

James recoiled at the sarcasm. "I didn't mean any offense, Ma'am."

"I don't think he meant it like that, Maggie." Doc called from across the room. "Don't be so jumpy."

James stared, wide eyed, at the Doc. He had no idea what he had said that was so bad.

Maggie sighed, "Sorry, James. There's a lot of disapproval back East against women doctors."

James looked at her, curiously. "Why? You can learn like everyone else, right?"

"Of course we can."

James shrugged, "Then why do they complain?"

"Because they think a woman can't do the job."

"Well that's dumb. Just 'cause you're a woman?"

Maggie had relaxed in her chair. "Yes, James. There are many that think women incapable." She shook her head, "I'm sorry I lashed out. I'm just used to backhanded questions."

"It's alright."

Doc stood stretching, and came into the kitchen to refill his coffee cup. "I've met a bunch of male doctors that have no business practicing medicine, but my Maggie... she's a natural." He beamed with pride. "She learned a lot when she would come to the clinic with me after her Mother died."

"Oh, I'm sorry." James turned back to Maggie, "I thought Mrs. Caroline was your Ma. How old were you when she passed?"

"I was six."

James nodded, "That's rough. My Ma passed when I was four, so I was raised by my Pa and my older brother." He grinned wide, "They didn't teach me no fancy doctoring though. It was plowing the garden and punching cows on the ranch."

"Well, they must have taught you something. You've ended up as the Sheriff."

James shrugged, "Well, not really. After the war I ended up going West for a while. Worked as a deputy in a few towns, and got some experience. When I came back last year, they offered me the job." He shrugged, "How about you? Why'd you want to keep doctoring? I mean, with all of the people throwing fits over it."

Maggie tilted her head to the side, "Well, I loved helping my father, and I was going to be a nurse. The reason I stayed east was to go to school for that. Then I started to get..." She shrugged, smiling, "Offended? I guess that's the word to use." She grinned, "I hate people telling me I can't do something."

"You'd better believe that." Doc laughed as he sat back down in his chair and picked up his book.

James grinned, "I can see that."

"Well, the woman who started the school I went to had really helped me. She had suffered through some of the same treatment for years, and wanted a place where women could learn without the backlash." She sighed, "There was still some, but not as much as I would've faced at another institution."

"Well, it's good that someone started a school like that. I think it's kind of dumb to cut someone off just because they are a woman."

Maggie looked surprised, "Really?"

He shrugged, "Well, there are some things I'm uncomfortable with a woman doing." He laughed briefly, "I arrested a cattle rustler in New Mexico that turned out to be a woman. She wore men pants and everything." He smiled at the memory, "She was better at roping cows than I am."

"Oh, my." Maggie laughed, "What happened to her? Is she still working with cattle?"

"Well, no..." James shrugged, sheepish. "Actually the Sheriff hung her."

"My Goodness, for stealing cows?"

"Yes Ma'am." He shook his head, "The point is, women working cattle, legally or not, is difficult for me. Doctoring and whatnot... nothing wrong with that."

"Interesting." Maggie leaned in, "So what do you think about a woman running for Congress?"

****

"Well, James, It was really good having you come out tonight." Doc had walked him out to the corral after dessert since he needed to get back to town.

James smiled, "I appreciate the invite."

Doc leaned in, conspiratorially, "Now see here." He whispered, looking around, "You and Maggie seemed to get on alright. She needs a good man in her life."

Startled by the boldness, James could only stare, wide eyed as Doc continued.

"I'd like to see more of you about, you know. Come out and visit more." He smiled broadly, "I think it'd do both of you some good." He patted James on the shoulder and chuckled, "It'd do me some good too."

"Well..." Awkwardly James searched for something to say, "I'll keep that in mind." He gestured to the sun, low in the western sky, "I'd better get heading toward town for now though. I wanted to get in before dark..." He let that sentence hang as he started saddling his horse.

"No problem young man. Have a safe ride back." Doc patted him on the shoulder one last time, and then ambled off toward the house.

James paused to watch him for a moment, and then hurriedly finished saddling his horse. He wanted to get going as quickly as possible.

****

James rode up the hill away from the Doc's house, amazed that he had survived the visit. That had been as awkward as a visit to Mrs. Johnson's.

He shook his head. Up 'til now people had seemed pretty... well, normal would've been the way he described them. Then two pretty girls come to town and everyone is all about his business.

It wasn't that he didn't like either one, they were both nice girls. He just wasn't sure he was ready to settle down.

He berated himself, it wasn't that he wasn't ready; it was that he wasn't prepared. He had always thought that settling down would be in the future, some far off thing that he would get to when he was older. Well, now he was older, and he had nothing to offer. Like he had told Earl, he made ten dollars a month and a bed in the jail. Maybe Earl was right. Maybe he needed to think about doing something else.

He sighed loudly. That was the problem with long rides, way too much time for thinking. He didn't really feel like considering all of his shortcomings for the entire ride home.

He had wanted to be home by dark, but it didn't look like that was going to happen.

He shifted his leg. It was throbbing a bit after the long day, probably from the constant bumping against his horse; it seemed like he had been in the saddle most of the day. He looked at the horizon, the sun was drooping toward the hills, and it was starting to get darker. He held his hand out at arm's length; he had half a fist, which was about half an hour 'til dark.

James clucked to his horse, goading it faster.

****

Chapter Sixteen

"**A**re you about ready?" Elizabeth's voice sounded through the door.

Catherine sighed before answering. She was still sitting on the bed, completely dressed and ready to go, just like she had been the last four times Elizabeth had asked. "Almost, just give me a minute." She looked across the room at the mirror and stared at her reflection, wondering if it were too late to just stay home sick.

Not that she was actually sick; she just dreaded facing James this morning. She had all but snubbed him the last few days, and she knew she needed to apologize.

She just wasn't really sure what to say.

It was just last week that the Lord had dealt with her about her self-will. The sermon that the Parson preached had really convicted her, and helped her realize that most of her problems had come from getting in front of the Lord. She committed to taking her decisions to the Lord and letting Him give her direction...

But, within a few days had completely blown it.

She had supposed that it was the tea with Maggie that brought it to the surface. In her mind coming West had been a temporary refuge; a place to get away from Alfred and all of the baggage that he had brought in her life. She had come here and got the help she needed, and as uncomfortable as that was, she was appreciative. For that, she loved it here.

But there were things about being out here that bothered her. The isolation, the separation from all of her other friends and family, and the infernal dust that was a major part of her life.

Simply put, there were things that she was looking forward to leaving behind. When Maggie had broached the possibility of her staying, it had scared her. She had thought that James might be interested in pursuing a relationship. As a matter of fact, there was a part of her that had been hoping for it. He was certainly attentive; even shy and charming all at the same time.

But there was that thing deep inside her, that sudden fear of how it would affect her plans to go back East. When he came into the store she... well, she was rude, and inconsiderate, and treated him horribly.

She had lain in bed last night for hours, unable to sleep as she considered how she had treated him. All he had ever done was show interest. She finally had to admit that the problem was with her. She had jumped into action when she thought that her plans weren't going the way she had wanted. She was getting ahead of the Lord. Again.

Once she finally admitted that the problem lie with her, she was able to take her frustrations to the Lord. She committed once more to allow the Lord to direct her life, and not try to direct it herself.

She had finally dropped off to sleep after that, content that she had cleared the air with the Lord and was on the right track. She had woke refreshed and invigorated, ready to go to Church.

Right up until she remembered that she was going to have to apologize to James for yesterday. She had been rude, and he deserved an apology.

And that was how she had ended up sitting on the bed for the past half an hour, staring at the mirror. She knew she needed to do it, but that wasn't helping her want to leave her room and go to Church. As a matter of fact, it was making her even more hesitant.

Frustrated, she knelt down on the edge of her bed and started praying.

****

James slowed to a walk as he entered the Church. He had ran late bringing Widow Johnson into town for Church. Her dog had been sick, and she had made him bathe it and put it in a bed before she would even leave the house. By the time they arrived at Church the song service was starting, but he'd had to unhitch the horses from the buckboard before running back to the jail to change clothes.

One thing he was certain of was that he was no longer partial to dogs.

He hurried to his pew, glad they were having longer music services nowadays. At least he hadn't missed the preaching. He scooted in the pew and sat down next to Thomas while they were singing a hymn.

"You're late, Mr. James." Thomas admonished quietly. He held his hymnal up so James could see it easier.

"I know. Thanks." He listened for a moment to see where they were in the song, and then joined in. His eyes drifted to the right, Catherine was focused on playing the piano. He watched her as she played, and wondered if she were still upset.

He was still curious as to why she was upset to begin with. He figured he would catch her after Church and ask her.

The song ended, and Ted moved back as the Parson came back to the pulpit.

James suppressed a chuckle as he remembered the meeting last week after Church, Widow Johnson had told the Parson he needed to stick to preaching, and that he needed to get someone behind the pulpit that could sing for song service. Parson had simply stared wide eyed as she shuffled out the door to the buckboard. He'd finally turned to James and shrugged, *"Well, I guess that means I need a song leader."*

Since everyone knew that the only person in the Church that sung worse than the Parson was James, he'd luckily been excused, and Ted had been assigned the exciting new role as song leader.

"Alright, friends,"

James shook off the memory and focused on the Parson.

"Let's open our Bibles to the Gospel of Matthew, chapter seven..."

****

Catherine looked down at her Bible, embarrassed that Anna had caught her staring.

Again.

She was trying to focus on the sermon, but her eyes kept drifting over to James. He was sitting in his usual spot with Thomas, his focus completely on the service.

She wished she could focus. Unfortunately, she had other things on her mind. She had been greeted outside by Maggie. She was in high spirits this morning, excited about James' visit last evening. She had nothing but good things to say about James, and how wonderful he was.

She felt a smile tug at her lips. So much for *'Not my type.'*

She had gotten some peace from the Lord after she had prayed earlier, and had come to Church with the intention of talking to James right off, but was disappointed when he hadn't got there before service started.

So now she had to wait, and think.

She had heard someone say once that giving an apology was like removing a splinter. Pulling it out always hurt, but the best way was to just yank it out and be done with it. That's what she wanted to do; yank it out and be done with it.

But instead she had to wait.

She mentally berated herself. She needed to pay attention to the service. She focused back on the Parson as he preached, and tried to keep her eyes from drifting back over to the third row where James was seated.

****

"Miss Catherine." James tipped his hat as Catherine stepped from the Church. He had stuck around after service to talk to her, but she had been inside for a long time talking to Anna in the back. He had waited outside for her; not that he had anything specific to say to her, but he just wanted to...

He really didn't know what he wanted to do. He felt dumb.

Catherine paused mid-step, "Oh, James. I'm so sorry. I didn't see you there."

He grinned, "Sorry, I didn't mean to startle you. Just wanted to say hello is all."

"Oh, yes. Hello." She looked back in the Church, "I was just heading to the house for dinner. We're having the Parson over, and I need to get things ready."

"Oh, that's fine." He gestured toward her house, "Want me to walk you there?"

She smiled, "That would be nice." She looked around, "Where's Widow Johnson?"

James sighed and rubbed his face with his hand. "She went to the Culpepper's for dinner." He was actually kind of happy about that, it meant he could eat his meal in peace today. As a bonus, Isaiah had even offered to take her home after they ate, which meant his afternoon was free.

"Oh, that's nice. They're nice people."

They both fell silent as they walked a few steps, then Catherine suddenly blurted out, "I'm sorry about yesterday."

"What do you mean?" James was fairly sure what she meant, but thought it was poor manners to say so.

"I just thought I may have been rude yesterday, and I wanted to say sorry."

James looked over at her and grinned, "Never noticed." He tried to think of something else to say; something that didn't involve the weather or people, but he couldn't think of anything.

"Why were you so late today, anyway?" She asked suddenly, rescuing him from his turmoil.

James shook his head, "You wouldn't believe me if I told you."

She tilted her head and smiled, "Try me."

****

Catherine watched through the window as James walked away from the house. He was a great storyteller when he got started. He had told her how messy he had gotten after giving Widow Johnson's dog a bath. She had thought she would never stop laughing.

She smiled softly, glad she had apologized. She had struggled through the rest of the Church service, not quite knowing how to approach him and not even sure if she could. By the time the service had ended she was at a complete loss, but Anna had stopped her. First, she scolded her for her lack of attention during the service, but when she explained her turmoil, Anna had given her that knowing half-smile and nodded. *"Well, make sure you talk to him then."*

And now, she was glad that she had.

She turned and looked at the clock on the mantle. Elizabeth had put on a couple of chickens for dinner, and they should be close to done. She needed to get finished before everyone else arrived.

****

Chapter Seventeen

"Sometimes I just don't understand womenfolk." James spoke suddenly, breaking the peaceful silence. He had rode out to the Parson's ranch early that morning to talk, and had just caught Parson and Thomas on their way to go fishing. Half an hour later the three of them were at the small lake trying to catch dinner.

The Parson smiled as he looked up from his fishing pole. "Are you saying there are times when you do understand them?"

Frowning, James nodded, then after considering it, started shaking his head. "No, I guess not." He watched his cork for a few moments. He had thought he'd seen it move. "It just seems like they sometimes make sense."

"Depends on the woman, I guess."

"That's true." The cork bumped slightly, not a bite, just a nip. "When it comes to courtin' and such though..."

"Are you getting married, Mr. James?"

Startled, James looked over. Thomas was watching him curiously. "Why would you ask that?"

"I was just wondering which one you were gonna pick."

"What?" Surprised, James recoiled, yanking his line through the water.

"You're scaring the fish." The Parson admonished.

"Sorry Parson." He looked back at Thomas. "What do you mean, pick?"

"Well," Thomas shrugged, "Seems like both Miss Catherine and Miss Maggie need a husband, and you need a wife. It can't work out for both of them, so I figured you were gonna pick."

"What makes you think I was gonna pick either one of them?"

"Why wouldn't you? They're both nice girls, aren't they?"

"Well, yes..."

"And neither one is already married."

"Not that I know of..."

"Then there's no reason you can't marry one of them." He shook his head sadly. "It's a shame you can't marry both though."

"What!" The Parson's head came up with that statement.

Thomas shrugged, "Well, Miss Catherine is more interesting, but she likes to hurt you a lot. It'd be nice if you had Miss Maggie to fix you up after."

James stared wide eyed for several seconds before shifting his gaze to the Parson. He had his hand over his face, fighting a losing battle with holding off his laughter.

"Well, Thomas, that's an interesting perspective." James offered. He knew Thomas was trying to help, but he just didn't...

"Do you know any poetry, Mr. James?" Thomas asked suddenly.

James blinked several times before answering. "No. No, I reckon not."

Thomas looked over, nodding sagely. "Mr. William told me I need to learn poetry so's I could catch a woman when I need to. You probably better learn some if you want to catch one of them."

"Not Keats." The Parson offered.

"Well, I'm not planning on checking into any poems just yet." James shook his head. "I just..." He had to admit, this whole thing had him frustrated.

And to think, it wasn't that many weeks ago that he had been happy, with no real problems, and no thought of women whatsoever.

"Thomas," The Parson suddenly spoke from the side, "Do me a favor and give us a minute."

"Yes sir." Thomas stood and pulled his line from the water, and then leaned the pole against a rock. He walked off slowly toward the other side of the lake.

James looked at the Parson questioningly. "What's up?"

"I figured it would be easier to talk without..." He gestured toward Thomas, "Little ears."

"Alright." He sighed and set his pole down. "Whatcha got for me?"

"Do you like her?"

"Who?"

The Parson rolled his eyes and shook his head. "Who? Oh, please tell me you're not going to play dumb about it."

James looked down at his pole. He knew the Parson was talking about Catherine, but hadn't really wanted to admit it. "I don't know. Maybe."

"Well, let me tell you something. You don't have to walk up to that little girl and ask her to marry you right off. Go sit on her porch, talk to her and get to know her better. I don't mean for a day or a week, but give it time. If the Lord leads you to move it further on, then you can cross that bridge when you come to it."

James nodded thoughtfully, he hadn't really thought of it like that. "You think she's interested in me enough to do that?" He shrugged, "I mean, she's been kind of..." He shrugged, "Back and forth."

"Probably because you haven't done that." The Parson shook his head, "A woman needs security. You're friendly, but is that as far as it goes? What do you talk about?"

"Well..."

The Parson shook his head sadly, "Please don't tell me you talk about yourself."

"I don't!"

"Good. Keep it that way. No woman likes a man that talks about himself all the time. Pick some things she'd want to talk about."

James nodded, listening intently. He just hoped he could remember all of this next time he saw her.

****

"I don't understand why you're so nervous. You're just asking permission to talk to her, not marry her." The Parson shook his head and grinned, "Well, not right off anyway." They had moved to the main room after dinner and were drinking coffee while Anna finished cleaning up after dinner

James took a sip of his coffee before answering, "That's easy for you to say. You didn't have to ask anyone before talking to Miss Anna."

"I had to pass your brother's scrutiny."

"Right, but Earl likes you. What if Ted says no? What do I do then?"

The Parson shook his head. "Do you really think that Ted is going to say no? He's the one that offered you a job as Sheriff."

"He might." He took the last drink of coffee and stared into his empty cup, "I know if I had a sister, I'd want someone with a tad more promise."

"Then ask him for a raise."

"Would either of you like some more coffee?"

James turned his head. Anna was in the kitchen, standing at the counter watching them. "No Ma'am. I'm going to have to get going. I still need to stop by Earl's on the way back." He stood and stretched. "That makes for a long ride."

The Parson chuckled and stood. "Well, I'm heading into town myself. I promised Jed Barlowe I'd come by and help him with the roof on the livery. Might as well do it today so I can hold your hand while you talk with Ted."

"Oh," Anna exclaimed, sounding pleased, "You're talking to Ted today? What about?"

"He wants permission to go sit on Ted's porch and talk."

"With Catherine? How sweet." Anna smiled at James, "I think she's a nice girl."

"Yeah, well he's nervous." The Parson chuckled, "I'll leave Thomas with you, that way if you need anything, he can get it."

"Alright William, that should be fine." She smiled, "Oh, and since you're going to be at the store anyway, bring me some tea."

"I will." He moved across the room and kissed her lightly on the cheek. "I'll try to be back by nightfall."

"That's fine," She looked over at James, "And you, don't be worrying. I'll be praying for you."

James nodded to Anna as he set his empty cup on the table, "Thank you, Ma'am. I appreciate the prayer."

They walked out to the barn and quickly saddled their horses. The Parson mounted easily and turned to James, "Take your time with Earl. I'll head straight in and take care of Jed. Holler at me when you get there."

****

"Ain't much of a town."

"Don't matter how big it is." Jensen replied testily, his face still pressed to his binoculars. "There's a store down there, which means the supplies that we need." He watched a few more minutes while Carter and Vic stared awkwardly at each other. He finally lowered the binoculars and grinned at them. "I don't see any sign of movement at the Jail. I think the Sheriff is gone."

"Are you sure?" Vic asked quietly. He was still shook up after Laramie. A deputy there had gotten awful nosey, and stopped them in the livery. Jensen had killed him and left the body buried under the dirty straw in the barn.

Jensen shrugged, "It'll be easy. We go in quickly, get the supplies we need, and get out."

Carter smiled humorlessly. He had to admit, Jensen had been right so far, and kept them ahead of the Marshal.

They knew there was a Deputy US Marshal on their trail. They had come across a few 'friends' of Jensen's who had filled them in. The Marshal had been trailing them for a few weeks now, but Jensen was always a step ahead of him.

Which was why he was still with Jensen.

"Alright, boys. In and out, no dilly-dallying. Get our supplies and we'll be in Colorado by tomorrow."

****

Catherine brushed the feather duster over the shelves. It was the third time so far today, but it was a mindless task that kept her occupied.

And one thing about this town, keeping occupied was the only thing that kept her from going crazy.

It wouldn't be so bad if she had someone to talk to all the time. The stores she shopped at in Philadelphia were always crowded with shoppers. On days that the stage came in she had a chance of getting some customers, but not always. As far as the locals, they were sporadic, only coming in when they needed something.

She had thought that she was going to be working side-by-side with her sister, but since she came to town, Elizabeth had taken to spending more time away from the store. Even Ted was often gone, and when he was here he was usually in the back, looking through catalogues for good deals to order. As a result, she spent most of her time alone, filling in time and waiting for a customer.

She glanced out the front window at the small, ugly building across the street, and wondered why James hadn't stopped by yet today. After their talk yesterday she had thought...

Well, she had thought he would at least come and visit.

She turned from the window and finished dusting the shelf. Her plans for the afternoon involved sitting down and starting on her new book. She had finished the poetry collection that Anna had given her, and was ready to start on another book she had brought; *A Christmas Carol*, which was written by a man named Charles Dickens. It was another one of Anna's favorites, so she had told her she would read it. She was getting to where she really enjoyed reading, which was fortunate since she had little else to do to pass time during the day.

Finishing up, she put the duster away and picked up the book. As soon as she sat down a horse whinnied on the street. She looked up, listening intently. She could hear horses coming up the street, and the low murmur of conversation.

She sighed and looked back down at her book. Whoever it was only had a one in three chance of stopping at the store, so she figured she would just start reading.

****

James had ridden away from Earl's nervously thinking about talking to Catherine. The Parson had given him some solid advice, and he hoped he could remember it all.

That was, if Ted was alright with him talking to Catherine to begin with.

He let his mind wander as he rode, trying to picture how his talk with Catherine would go. He thought she might be interested, but you never really knew.

It was like his Pa used to say. Women could be contrary critters.

A cool breeze had sprung up as he rode. It had been getting steadily cooler for the last week or so, and he knew that fall was right around the corner. He could see that some of the trees were already starting to turn, so it wouldn't be long before the riot of color turned to winter.

He quickened his pace, wanting to get back to town in plenty of time to talk with Ted...

And then Catherine. He wasn't sure which one made him more nervous.

He still struggled with his future, and how that was going to affect this relationship. That was why he had stopped to talk to Earl. He couldn't stay on as Sheriff forever. He was eventually going to have to do something else. Earl wanted him to take over the ranch, but he wasn't sure. One of the main struggles he had faced was what that would mean for the town. He had been honored when they offered him the job as Sheriff, but deep down he knew there wasn't a long line of applicants for the position. Nobody could really afford to, not at ten dollars a month. He was going to have to do something different. If he ever did get hitched, he was sure that his wife wouldn't enjoy living in the jail. That would be pretty awkward.

As he got near to town he slowed some, trying to plan out how he was going to approach Catherine.

"Whoa..." He pulled up his horse and stared at the edge of the road. He could see where a set of tracks had left the road, and were riding across the field.

Curious, James nudged the horse with his heel, pulling the reins to the side to follow the tracks. The town lay sprawled out below, just visible over the lip of the hill. The tracks followed a circuitous route just past the edge of the hill. He followed them around slowly, growing concerned as the tracks crossed the road leaving town and continued across. He stopped a few feet from the road and dismounted, leading his horse over to the trail.

James squatted down, looking closely at the tracks. There were three horses, and they were keeping a wide berth around town. Standing, he looked around, noting that the trail stayed right past the lip of the hill, which would keep the riders out of view of the town below. He knew that anyone passing through would have rode through town, not a circle around it.

That is, unless they didn't want to be spotted. He frowned, mounting his horse, nudging him closer to the edge so he could look down the hill. He could see the town below, looking peaceful in the afternoon sun.

He could also see several horses tied in front of the store. It could be nothing, but...

****

Chapter Eighteen

Catherine knew something was wrong from the moment the three men entered the store. One of them, a twitchy looking one, stayed by the door while the other two fanned out, moving through the store. She forced a smile and asked, "May I help you, gentlemen?"

The men ignored her as they checked the store. She moved to the other side of the counter, closer to the pistol, watching them closely as they looked around.

"Where's the Sheriff?"

She turned, startled. The twitchy one by the door was staring hard. He gestured outside, "Where's the Sheriff? He wasn't at the jail."

Catherine thought fast. The last thing she wanted was for them to think that James wasn't around. "I'm not sure, he must be somewhere around. Is there something I can do?"

A deep voice growled behind her, "You can step away from that gun you have under the counter, missy."

She turned slowly, one of the others had moved up behind her, and was pointing a pistol at her. He looked vaguely familiar, but she couldn't place him right off...

"Move!" He demanded again, startling her into action. She stepped quickly away from the counter and lifted her hands.

"What's going on?"

They all turned at the same time. Ted had stepped into the store from the back room, a puzzled look on his face. The man with the pistol shifted, and pointed it at Ted. "Hand's up."

"Whoa there." Ted held his hands up, palms out. "Look gentlemen, we don't want any trouble..."

"Shut up!" The third one snapped. He had been looking through the store, and had come up behind Ted with a cut down double barrel shotgun that he must have pulled from his coat. "Move and I'll spread you across the floor."

"She said she didn't know where the Sheriff was, Jensen." The twitchy one whined from his spot by the door.

"Then keep an eye out you fool. If he comes in, shoot him." He turned to the one aiming the pistol at Ted, "Carter, get moving on those supplies."

Catherine felt her blood run cold when the twitchy one called the one man Jensen. She watched him, her eyes wide with fear as he moved through the store. She had heard too much about him to think this was going to end well.

"Just take what you want." Ted offered.

The one with the pistol, Carter, hadn't moved, but was staring at her. "Hey Jensen. I remember her now. I rode the stage in with her. Remember, I told you about her."

Catherine had a flash of recognition as she recalled the smelly businessman from the stage.

Jensen moved up from behind Ted and grinned, "That uppity one you had talked about?" He leered openly at her, "Yeah, I remember." He shook his head, "Get the supplies first, then we'll worry about her."

****

James rode down the hill at a slow canter. He didn't want anyone to hear him coming, just in case. There was a part of him that hoped this was nothing, but deep down he knew something was off. His eyes narrowed as he focused on the front of the store, watching for movement. As he neared the corral he was surprised when the Parson stepped from behind the livery, holding his hand up.

"Whoa there, James. Glad you finally got here."

James slowed and angled his horse toward the livery, pulling the horse to a stop around the corner, hidden from view of the store. "How's it look?"

The Parson shook his head grimly, "Not good. Three men rode into town acting skittish and nervous. They stopped at the livery and knocked Jed Barlowe out and left him trussed up in a stall." He jerked a thumb behind him, "He's alive, but still out. I saw them just come out of the jail, but then they went into the store. I was heading around when I saw you coming down the hill."

Dismounting quickly, James pulled his rifle from the scabbard. He peeked around the corner at the store, and then blew out a long breath. "Got a plan, then?"

"Well, at three to one I felt it best to just kill them all. Did you want to try an arrest?"

James turned and looked hard at the Parson. Coming from anyone else, it would have seemed like false bravado, or even arrogance... but they had fought in the war together. James knew better. "If they go easy, take them without shooting to keep the others safe." He shook his head slowly, "But if not..." He trailed off.

The Parson nodded. "Yeah." He moved up to the corner and pointed. "I'll go straight for the front and get them to focus on me..."

James held up his hand, stopping him. "That's way too dangerous if they come out shooting."

The Parson grinned wide, "They wouldn't shoot a man with a clerical collar, would they?" He shook his head, "No, I'll take the front, and you go around..." A scream from the store echoed up the street. The Parson clasped James' shoulder, "You know what to do. You better move."

****

Catherine shook uncontrollably as she watched the twitchy one dance back as he looked out the front window. She couldn't tell who was more scared, him or her. He turned to Jensen, his face tight, "We need to get out of here. You said in and out. Let's just take what we got and go."

They had already retrieved several sacks of food and other goods, and had moved them to the door. Ted had even opened the safe, allowing them to take everything in the hopes that they would just leave. As Jensen moved closer to the door, he paused, staring again at Catherine as she stood silently by the counter. "You sure you don't want to come with us, missy?" He leered suggestively at her again.

Before she could stop herself, Catherine spat, "Shut up, you pig!"

"Hang on." Carter had come up behind her and shoved Catherine away from the counter and into the wall. "I don't recall asking you to call us names." He pressed Catherine against the wall and traced the muzzle of his pistol down her cheek. "You know, Jensen," He spoke over his shoulder, "I was right. This one is too uppity." He grinned, baring his teeth, reminding her of a rabid wolf. "Since she thinks she's better than us, we oughta take her with us and teach her to treat people right."

Jensen shrugged, "Whatever, let's just hurry."

Catherine took a deep breath, her eyes wide with terror. She looked at Ted, silently pleading with him for help. Carter pulled her from the wall, and shoved her toward the front door. "Let's go, Miss Uppity."

"That'll be enough of that!" Ted stepped forward and reached toward Carter, but Jensen stepped forward and swung his shotgun in a short, chopping motion and caught Ted across the temple. He dropped immediately to the floor, unconscious.

Catherine screamed and moved to help Ted. The whole side of his face was covered in blood. She knelt, but was suddenly yanked backwards, and flung against the counter. She caught her balance, and found herself staring into the muzzle of Carter's pistol.

"Now, let's get moving." He grabbed her by her shoulder and shoved her roughly toward the door.

"How are you going to get her on a horse?" Vic whined from the door.

Jensen growled, "He can flop her over his saddle. Do you have the money?"

"Yeah."

Catherine felt Carter's pistol in the small of her back. "Don't you try to run off now, Miss Uppity," He warned. He opened the door and shoved her through, following closely behind.

The sun blinded her as she stumbled out onto the boardwalk, she could feel its burning heat as he shoved her toward the steps. She looked left and right for an escape, but she was shaking so badly that she could barely keep her feet. She wondered if Ted was dead, or...

"Hold it right there!"

Her breath caught as she heard Parson William's voice from the street. She turned and looked. He stood in the center of the street, his left hand out in a halting gesture.

"Look boys, it's a Sky Pilot!" Jensen laughed from the side, having come out of the store last.

"Get out of here, Parson, unless you want to be hurt too." Carter snarled from behind her. He still had his pistol pressed into her back.

The Parson held his ground. "I can't let you do that, boys. Let the lady go."

A cackling laugh sounded from her left. The twitchy one had stepped up, leering. Even he was brave against an unarmed...

Wait! The Parson was never unarmed. Was he going to...?

A loud voice growled from the other end of the boardwalk. "Put down your guns and nobody dies."

She swiveled her head, James stood at the far end of the boardwalk, a large rifle pointed in their direction.

Carter yanked her close, his arm across her throat. He pointed his pistol over her shoulder toward James. "No, Sheriff, you need to drop that gun, right now, or the lady dies."

The stale smell of sweat was making her gag reflexively. Carter pushed her forward toward James.

"Last chance boys, or else." James warned, not moving.

Twitchy cackled again, "Last chance for..."

Catherine jumped at the sound of a shot.

****

James had moved around the side of the restaurant to cut the gang off. They were focused on the Parson. He had come across the middle of the street, in plain view, hoping to distract them.

So far it was working.

James took a sharp breath and stepped around the corner of the building, facing the men. His lips tightened as he leveled his rifle. He considered taking the shot, but worried he would hit Catherine. He figured he would try diplomacy first. "Put down your guns and nobody dies."

The one that was holding Catherine spun to face him. He pulled Catherine close, like a shield, and aimed his pistol over her shoulder. "No, Sheriff, you need to drop that gun, right now, or the lady dies."

James stood his ground, mentally evaluating the threat. He focused briefly on the man holding Catherine, and then shifted his eyes; briefly taking in the next two. The one closest to him was scared, putting a show on for the others. He wouldn't move unless the others did. The one with Catherine thought he held the cards... his eyes flickered to the Parson. He had him.

The one that worried him the most was the one behind the nervous one, the one closest to the door. He could tell by the way he looked that he wasn't right in the head, and that was dangerous. He was hanging back, shielding himself behind the nervous one.

James knew that it was going to end up in a shootout really quick. He could see the Parson angling closer. He needed to keep their attention on himself. He shook his head "Last chance boys, or else."

The nervous one by the door started to talk, but the Parson, forgotten by the gang, had slipped within a few feet of the one holding Catherine. He nodded once, and then stepped forward, drew and fired at the man from point blank range.

The street exploded in action.

Everyone moved at once. The one holding Catherine fell away from her, stumbling back toward the store's front window as the Parson continued firing into him. James saw Catherine drop, but then the twitchy one leaped sideways and turned his pistol toward the Parson. James triggered a quick shot into him, then levered his rifle and shot again.

James felt a harsh jolt as something slammed into his right shoulder. He staggered back into a support post and dropped his rifle from the shock.

He felt the heat of a second blast past his face that would have hit him if he hadn't fallen back. Struggling to right himself, he spotted the man behind the twitchy one moving toward him, mechanically reloading a double barrel shotgun.

Guns were still hammering around him, but James focused on the man with the shotgun. He reached across his body with his left hand, and awkwardly drew his pistol. As he struggled upright he fired twice in rapid succession, striking the man in the side. James watched the man's body jerk with each hit, but he finished putting the shells in the shotgun and closed the breech.

James reached his feet and fired again, but the man stood firm, slowly bringing the shotgun up for another shot. James took a step to one side and shot twice more, both rounds striking the man in the chest as the shotgun leveled and fired.

****

Catherine lay paralyzed with fear on the boardwalk as the guns stopped firing. As soon as Carter had let go of her, she had dove to the ground and watched the Parson walk forward, fanning the hammer on his pistol, the orange tongue of flame leaping out toward her as each shot, one after the other, found its mark, smashing Carter further away from her.

"Are you alright?"

She lifted her head; the Parson was thumbing shells into his pistol as he moved toward her. "Catherine? Are you hit?"

"I'm fine." She muttered slowly. She turned her head slightly, recoiling at the sight of blood that covered the boardwalk. The twitchy one lay sprawled out against the side of the bench she liked to sit on, his leg bent at an unnatural angle. Turning her head further, she spotted Jensen; he was leaning against the building, his eyes wide open and staring, obviously dead.

She felt a wave of relief surge through her that stopped when she noticed the still form on the boardwalk just past Jensen.

She surged to her feet and rushed forward. James was lying further down the boardwalk, a pool of blood slowly spreading from his still form.

****

As Carter lay dying on the boardwalk, he looked over at Jensen's body. His last thought was that they should've cut loose of Jensen long before.

****

Chapter Nineteen

"...he going to live?"

James blinked himself awake, struggling to remember why he would be lying down in the first place. He stared at the ceiling, but it was blurry and out of focus. He could hear the low murmur of conversation across the room. He blinked a few more times and turned his head, finally recognizing the jail. Doc, his daughter, and the Parson were talking in low tones by the window. He tried to sit up, but a wave of dizziness and pain made him sink back onto his pillow. He closed his eyes for a second; the light was so bright in the room that it had burned his eyes as he tried to focus.

He waited for the dizziness to pass, and then forced himself up to a sitting position. He looked over at the Parson and tried to clear his throat, but could only rasp out a weak growl. The Parson finally noticed him sitting and grinned, gesturing for the others to look. "Well, look who decided to wake up."

"What happened?" He barely got the words out before he started coughing, the spasms sending wracking pain through his entire right side.

Maggie hurried over and grabbed a cup of water from the small table, putting the cup to his lips, "Here, drink this."

He sipped slowly, and then nodded gratefully as she pulled the cup away.

"Is that better?" She asked quietly, her face showing concern.

"Yeah." James rasped, and then looked questioningly at the Parson and blinked a few times as his memory returned. "Catherine?"

"She's fine. She just left a half hour ago, been worrying about you the whole time."

James scrunched up his face as he tried to remember, "I saw her go down..."

"She passed out in fright." The Parson shrugged, "A couple of men died within inches of her. That might be traumatic."

James nodded slowly, "What about the others?" He rubbed his face with his palm, and tried to swing his feet out to the floor.

"Whoa there..." Maggie grabbed his shoulder, "You don't need to get up."

"Just sit back, James." Doc finally spoke from his spot by the window. "There is no reason to get up."

He stayed sitting until Maggie, sighing in frustration, pushed a pillow behind his back. He relaxed and leaned back onto the pillow.

"And to answer your question, they're all dead. That's how you ended up here." The Parson shook his head in mock sadness, "You fell into the sin of greed and laziness. You tried to take two by yourself and ended up taking a few hits, and now you've been lollygagging in bed since yesterday."

James started to chuckle at the dry humor, and ended up coughing instead. He gasped at the pain in his chest as he finally got the cough under control and rasped out, "You send someone to report it?"

The stage came through earlier. Ray's going to telegraph the U.S. Marshal when he gets to Dana."

"That'll work." He flexed his shoulder, wincing at the pain. He was sore all over. He looked over at the Doc who was standing quietly by the window, "How bad was it?"

Doc looked up and shrugged, "We pulled twelve pieces of buckshot from you. That scattergun was about the end of you." He gestured to the Parson,

"He was right, greed will get you. You had more holes than anyone else on the street. Nine in your shoulder and chest, two in your arm, and one in your hip." He grinned, "And I didn't count the one that grazed that hard head of yours."

"How long do I need to be here?"

Doc laughed, "Well, normally I'd say two weeks, minimum, but that means you'll be pushing to get up by tomorrow."

****

Catherine was still kneeling in her pew when she heard the door open in the back of the Church. She had been quietly praying alone for the last few minutes, trying to keep her mind off of the fear that she felt every time she heard a horse, every time she heard a step...

Every time she looked at James and thought he might die.

It was hard to describe what she was going through. She had tried to talk to Elizabeth after it was all over, but she couldn't. It wasn't until Anna got there later that evening that she could finally share some of it.

She had never seen someone die before. She had been to funerals, but those people had been prepared, not spraying blood everywhere. Even with that though, after what she had gone through... she was glad those men were dead. Deep down she had known that James would save her, but it wasn't until he had appeared around the corner that she let herself believe.

And now he was lying down the street, laid out in a bed ready to die. Unless that was what someone was here to tell her, that he had already died.

"Are you alright?"

At the sound of the voice, Catherine looked up. Anna was standing a few feet away, concern etched on her face.

"Is he dead?"

Anna recoiled, obviously confused, "James? No. I just wanted to check on you."

Catherine sighed and rested her cheek on the pew. "I'm fine, I guess. I just..." She trailed off with a gesture and closed her eyes for a few seconds before finishing, "I guess I just want to go home. Nothing like this ever happened there."

"I understand that. I felt the same way after Clay passed, like the further away I got from here the better I'd be."

Catherine felt the tears well up in her eyes. Somehow knowing that someone else knew how she felt was so... it was indescribable.

"But, what I finally understood," Anna continued after a brief pause, "Was that bad things happen everywhere you go."

Catherine lifted her head to look at Anna.

"You see," Anna gestured outside, "They say that lightning never hits the same place twice. That is not entirely true, but it's true enough to think about. If you are at a tree that just got hit, you shouldn't run to another, because that may be the next place it hits."

"So, you're saying I shouldn't go?"

Anna opened her mouth to answer when the door of the Church opened. "There you are." Maggie's voice filled the sanctuary, "Someone's awake and asking about you, Catherine."

****

James looked up from his Bible as the door opened and Catherine poked her head through the door. She smiled, uncomfortably, "Are you awake?"

He smiled, "Yeah, come on in. You just missed the rest of them though. They said something about getting some dinner at Maude's."

"Are you sure I'm not bothering you?"

"Of course not," He closed his Bible, "They wanted me to sleep, but I think I've slept too much." He nodded down at the Bible on his lap, "I was just reading."

She came into the room, closing the door softly behind her. She looked skeptically around the jail, "Are you sure you're comfortable here?"

He grinned weakly, "Well, the bunk in the cell is fairly uncomfortable, but my bed's good. So's that chair." He gestured to the chair next to his bed, "Have a seat."

She smiled awkwardly and sat, "I just wanted to check on you. Maggie told us you were awake." She shrugged, "I came over last night, but you were sleeping."

"Yeah, Doc wants me to be sleeping now." He chuckled lightly, but then broke into a coughing spell.

"Oh, I'm so sorry!" Catherine stood, but he waved his hand for her to sit back down.

"I'm fine." He breathed, clearing his throat, "Just a tad raspy."

"I didn't want to bother you," She sat quietly for a few moments, staring at her hands before continuing, "I just wanted to say thank you. I was so scared..." She trailed off.

"It's no problem, really."

Catherine shook her head slowly, "I don't know. I was talking to Anna earlier. I'm not sure if I'm cut out for this. I told her that I was thinking about going back East."

"Oh." He frowned, leaning back against his pillow. He didn't really know what to say at this point, he didn't know if he should argue, beg, or just keep quiet.

They sat there in silence while he tried to think of something to say, but nothing sounded right. After a few minutes she stood, "I'm sorry I bothered you."

"Wait." He rubbed his face with his hand, this had seemed so much easier when he thought about talking to her on that ride home, what was it, yesterday? He shook his head, "I just want to..." He was bad at this. "I don't want you to go."

Catherine sat back down in the chair, confused, "I can stay if you need me..."

James blew out a long breath. He needed to just get it over with, "No, I mean I don't want you to go back East." He blushed, and looked back down at the Bible in his lap, "I was riding home yesterday, before the..." he trailed off, shrugging, "Anyway, I was gonna talk to you." He looked up, "Well, I was gonna talk to Ted first, but I was gonna ask you if you'd be interested in sittin' on the porch to talk." He groaned inwardly, now he probably sounded like a fool.

She looked at him curiously, "About what?"

He blew out another breath. Yep, she thought he was dumb, he better just get it done. "You know, getting to know more about each other."

She stared at him blankly for a few moments before understanding lit her face. "Oh, you mean, like courting?"

"Well, yes ma'am."

She smiled softly, "James, nothing would make me happier."

****

Epilogue

James leaned his chair back against the wall as he enjoyed the gentle evening breeze. The setting sun had turned the entire valley a dull orange color. He sighed, relaxing his body. He was still supposed to be in bed, the Doc had about lost his mind when he saw him up this morning.

He smiled as he remembered the look on his face, "You just took the equivalent of twelve rounds two days ago you fool, get back in bed and get some rest."

He was getting rest, he just couldn't stay flat on his back to do it. Even Maggie had partially agreed, much to Doc's annoyance. Something about not getting pneumonia...

His eyes caught a flicker of movement. A rider had topped out on the hill above town and was riding slowly down the road. James shifted his leg, putting his pistol in an easier position.

Just in case.

He watched the rider as he came down the trail. As he got closer he noticed that the man was slumped over the saddle. He leaned his chair back forward and stood gingerly, scanning the hills around for movement. He had to admit, he was a tad paranoid after the other day.

The horse continued down the trail and into town. James clicked his tongue and the horse responded immediately, moving toward him. He could tell the rider was unconscious now, and had tied himself to the saddle. He stepped lightly from the porch, and yelled toward the store, "Hey, Ted!"

As the horse neared, he grabbed the bridle, and tied the horse to the hitching post before looking at the rider. He heard the door across the street crash open, "What's going on, Sheriff?"

Moving to the side of the horse, James tapped the rider's leg. No response. "Got a man hurt, Ted." He yelled.

Ted ran across the street, "I'll get him down."

James held the horse still while Ted cut the cords the rider had bound himself to the saddle with, and then slowly let him down to the ground.

"Uh, oh," Ted muttered quietly.

James looked around the horse at the rider that was lying on the ground. The first thing that stuck out was the shiny silver badge on his chest that distinctly read, 'Deputy U.S. Marshal.'

****

Also Available

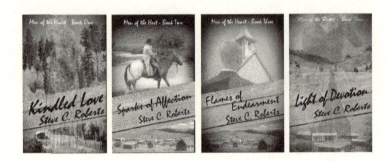

Read the rest of the series, now available in eBook and print.

About the Author

STEVE C. ROBERTS lives in Central Missouri with his wife and four children. He is a professional teacher and counselor, and has spent the last twenty-five years in the prison ministry. He also serves in various other capacities in his home Church. His writings include several Non-fictional devotionals as well as several Christian Fiction novels, including the Men of the Heart series.

Made in the USA
Monee, IL
19 March 2022